Thomas Hood

Humorous Poems

Thomas Hood

Humorous Poems

ISBN/EAN: 9783744765169

Printed in Europe, USA, Canada, Australia, Japan

Cover: Foto ©Andreas Hilbeck / pixelio.de

More available books at **www.hansebooks.com**

HUMOROUS POEMS

BY

THOMAS HOOD

WITH A PREFACE BY

ALFRED AINGER

AND ONE HUNDRED AND THIRTY ILLUSTRATIONS

BY

CHARLES E. BROCK

London

MACMILLAN AND CO.

AND NEW YORK

1893

PREFACE

SOME time in the year 1825 there was published in London a thin duodecimo volume having for title Odes and Addresses to Great People. *It bore no author's name on the title-page,—only a quotation from the* Citizen of the World, *" Catching all the oddities, the whimsies, the absurdities and the little-nesses of conscious greatness by the way."* The little *book proved, on examination, to contain some fifteen humorous poems addressed to various public characters of greater or less claim to distinction at that day. There was one to Mr. Graham, the aeronaut; another to M'Adam, the maker of roads; another to Mrs. Fry, the Quaker philanthropist; another to Grimaldi, the clown, and so forth. An acute critic might, even then, I think, have detected not only that these fresh and amusing productions were of unequal*

merit, but that they were not all by the same hand.
But he would, most assuredly, have allowed that wit
and ingenuity of a rare kind were to be found among
them.

The little volume quickly attracted attention, and
was soon in a second edition. Among those into
whose hands it fell was Samuel Taylor Coleridge,
then residing under Mr. Gillman's roof at Highgate.
His delight was great; and in the absence of any in-
formation as to the authorship, he at once assumed that
such mingled fun and poetry could have emanated from
but one living man—and that, the author of Elia.
Accordingly Coleridge wrote off at once to Charles
Lamb :—

MY DEAR CHARLES—This afternoon a little thin mean-
looking sort of a foolscap sub-octavo of poems, printed on very
dingy outsides, lay on the table, which the cover informed me
was circulating in our book-club, so very Grub Streetish in all
its appearance, internal as well as external, that I cannot
explain by what accident of impulse (assuredly there was no
motive in play) I came to look into it. Least of all the title,
Odes and Addresses to Great Men, which connected itself in
my head with Rejected Addresses, and all the Smith and
Theodore Hook squad. But, my dear Charles, it was certainly
written by you, or under you, or unâ cum you. I know none
of your frequent visitors, capacious and assimilative enough of
your converse, to have reproduced you so honestly, supposing

you had left yourself in pledge in his lock-up house. Gillman, to whom I read the spirited parody on the Introduction to Peter Bell, the Ode to the Great Unknown, and to Mrs. Fry—he speaks *doubtfully of Reynolds and Hood. . . .*

Thursday night, 10 o'clock—*No! Charles, it is* you! *I have read them over again, and I understand why you have* anoned *the book. The puns are nine in ten good—many excellent,—the* Newgatory, *transcendent! And then the* exemplum sine exemplo *of a volume of personalities and contemporaneities without a single line that could inflict the infinitesimal of an unpleasance on any man in his senses—saving and except, perhaps, in the envy-addled brain of the despiser of your* Lays. *If not a triumph over him, it is, at least, an* Ovation. *Then moreover and besides (to speak with becoming modesty), excepting my own self, who is there but you who could write the musical lines and stanzas that are intermixed?*

Lamb writes back on the second of July from Colebrooke Row, Islington, and after telling Coleridge of his own recent illness and the weariness of being without occupation—he had just retired from the India House—he proceeds :—

The Odes are, four-fifths, done by Hood—a silentish young man you met at Islington one day, an invalid. The rest are Reynolds's, whose sister Hood has lately married. I have not had a broken finger in them. . . . Hood will be gratified, as much as I am, by your mistake.

And Lamb is able to add at the close of his

letter : " Hood has just come in ; his sick eyes sparkled with health when he read your approbation."

The " silentish young man—an invalid" was then just six-and-twenty years of age.   He had been forced to abandon, for health's sake, the engraver's desk to which he had been bound ; had become in 1821 sub-editor of the London Magazine, *and in that service, and at the hospitable table of the publishers, Taylor and Hessey, had both practised his poetic gift and made the most valuable and inspiring friendships of his life,—with Hazlitt, De Quincey, Hartley Coleridge, and, above all, in Hood's affection and admiration, Charles Lamb, then just beginning to contribute his essays to the magazine.   One greater genius than any in the list it was not given to Hood to know in the flesh.   John Keats had closed his brief life of suffering at Rome in the February of the year in which Hood joined the staff.   But it was under the spell of that poetic genius that Hood began his career as poet. Among the friends he owed to the magazine was John Hamilton Reynolds, his future brother-in-law. Reynolds had been one of Keats's closest friends, and himself wrote verse of considerable merit, bearing strong marks of the Keatsian influence.   Hood remained sub-editor for two or three years, and contributed many of his longer serious poems, clearly due in subject as well as style to the same influence— his " Lycus the Centaur," " The Two Peacocks of Bedfont," the " Ode to Autumn," and others. But very early in his editorial. career he had also printed in the magazine, modestly, among certain imaginary and whimsical " Notices to Correspondents," a short and facetious " Ode to Dr. Kitchener," prelude and model of those which afterwards so captivated Coleridge. But this, with all other of Hood's contributions at this time, was anonymous, and together with the serious poetry, seems to have attracted scant notice. Unsigned poetry, even seventy years ago, was sufficiently abundant, and, for the most part, sufficiently commonplace, for the general reader to pass it by as so much padding. And when the* Odes and Addresses, *the joint-production of Hood and Reynolds, appeared anonymously in 1825, even those who lived in the world of literature were in some doubt as to the authorship.*

In 1824 Hood married Jane Reynolds, contrary, it would seem, to the wishes of her family ; and indeed, with his health and uncertain prospects, the match may well have been deemed imprudent. In any case the "bread and cheese" question had become urgent. The Odes and Addresses *came out in the year following, to be soon followed by the two series of* Whims and Oddities; *and in 1827 Hood reprinted his Serious Poems from the* London Magazine *with some new matter, including the graceful poem which gave its name to the volume, "The Plea of the Midsummer Fairies." This poem was dedicated to Charles Lamb,—the volume, as a whole, to Coleridge, in grateful recognition of the praise he had bestowed on Hood's earlier efforts,—but neither poems nor dedications availed to awaken any interest in the reading public. The volume fell all but dead from the press; and the author, his son and daughter tell us, bought up a large number of the remainder copies, "to save them from the butter-shop."*

It now became evident that if Hood was to live by writing, it must be by his humorous, not his serious verse; and though happily his poetic genius was not discouraged, the remaining eighteen years of his life were spent mainly in working that rich and unique vein of which he had given earliest proof in his Odes and Addresses. *He was to show that in the hands*

*of a poet and humorist, the pun—that so-called " verbal
wit"—was to take higher rank and subserve quite other
purposes than anything of the kind in our literature
before.   Samuel Johnson once remarked that "little
things are not valued, but when they are done by those
who can do greater things."   But he might have gone
further, and said that the little things only* become
*great when they proceed from those who can do greater,
—who come to them, that is to say, from a higher
ground.*

*And, with Hood, this higher ground was the poetic
heart, and a vividness and rapidity of imagination
such as never before had found such an outlet.   The
same instantaneous perception of the analogies and
relations between, apparently, incongruous things that
was possessed by Dickens, Hood possessed with regard
to words and ideas.   The pun, as ordinarily understood, is a play upon the double meanings of words, or
on the resemblance of one word to another; and in the
hands of one destitute of humour or fancy the pun
begins and ends there.   It may be purely mechanical,
and if so, speedily becomes wearisome and disgusting.
To hear of any ordinary man that he makes puns is
properly a warning to avoid his society.   For with the*

*funny man the verbal coincidence is everything ; there
is nothing underlying it, or beyond it. In the
hands of a Hood the pun becomes an element in his
fancy, his humour, his ethical teaching, even his
pathos. As ordinarily experienced, the pun is the irre-
concilable enemy of these things. It could not dwell
with them " in one house." Hood saw, and was the
first to show, that the pun might become even their
handmaid, and in this confidence dared to use it often
in his serious poems, when he was conveying some
moral truth, or expressing some profound human
emotion. Coleridge, as we have seen, remarking on
the excellence of the puns in the* Odes and Addresses,
added, "The Newgatory *is transcendent !" Hood was
addressing the admirable Mrs. Fry, who, as every one
knows, set up a school in Newgate to teach the poor
neglected outcasts what they had never heard from
Christian lips before. One of the chief points made
by Hood is this,—how much better, kinder, wiser, more
politic even, it would be to multiply these schools*
outside, *not* inside *the Prison walls, so that pre-
vention might take the place of cure. "Keep your
school out of Newgate" is the burden of Hood's
remonstrance :—*

Ah! who can tell how hard it is to teach
Miss Nancy Dawson on her bed of straw—
To make Long Sal sew up the endless breach
She made in manners—to write heaven's own law
On hearts of granite; nay, how hard to preach,
In cells, that are not memory's—to draw
The moral thread thro' the immoral eye
Of blunt Whitechapel natures, Mrs. Fry!

*And then, after a stanza or two, comes the one
ending with the play on words that so fascinated
Coleridge :—*

I like your chocolate, good Mistress Fry!
I like your cookery in every way;
I like your Shrove-tide service and supply:
I like to hear your sweet Pandeans *play;*
I like the pity in your full-brimmed eye;
I like your carriage, and your silken grey,
Your dove-like habits, and your silent preaching;
But I don't like your Newgatory *teaching!*

*The distinctive quality of Hood's puns is exempli-
fied here, but not more notably than in a hundred other
instances that crowd upon the memory. The ordinary
pun is, for the most part, profoundly depressing, being
generally an impertinence ; while Hood's at their best
exhilarate and fill the reader with a glow of admiration and surprise. The " sudden glory " which Hobbes
pronounced to be the secret of the pleasure derived from
wit is true of Hood's. There was a pretty drawing-*

room ballad by his brother-in-law Reynolds, which
our grandmothers used to sing to an equally pretty
tune, beginning—

> Go where the water glideth gently ever,
>   Glideth by meadows that the greenest be ;
> Go, listen to our own belovèd river
>   And think of me !

Hood had a young lady friend who was going to
India, and he writes her a playful copy of verses, imi-
tating Reynolds's poem in metre and refrain.   Hood
noticed that the matrimonial market, already in his
day, was somewhat overstocked, and that watchful
parents had the comfort of hoping that daughters who
lingered in England might yet find husbands in the
smaller society of Bombay or Madras, and he adds—

> Go where the maiden on a mariage plan goes,
> Consigned for wedlock to Calcutta's quay,
> Where woman goes for mart, the same as mangos,
>   And think of me !

The same as man goes !   How utter the
surprise, and yet how inevitable the simile appears !
It is just as if the writer had not foreseen it—as if
it had been mere accident—as if he had discovered
the coincidence rather than arranged it.   This is
a special note of Hood's best puns.   They fall

into their place so obviously, like the rhymes of a
consummate lyrist, that it would have seemed
pedantic to go out of the way to avoid them. The
verses in the present collection supply instances in
abundance. Every one remembers Lieutenant Luff's
apology for his particular weakness in respect of
stimulants—

> If wine's a poison, so is Tea,
>   Though in another shape :
> What matter whether one is kill'd
>   By canister, or grape !

In another poem here given, and less known
(suggested. by Burns's Twa Dogs), the Pointer bitterly
complains that his master is such a novice that he
never hits a bird, and that now he has taken to
a double-barrel the "aggravation" is worse than
before :—

> And now, as girls a-walking do,
> His misses go by two and two !

In these last-quoted jests the purpose is, of course,
humorous and fantastic, and is little more ; but Hood
never hesitated to make the pun minister to higher
ends, and vindicate its right to a share in quickening
men's best sympathies. An apparently little known
copy of verses will be found in the present volume,

b

written to support an "Early Closing Movement" of
Hood's day, in which his interest was keen as it was
in all proposed remedies for suffering and oppression.
It seems strange that the verses have never been
reprinted in behalf of grievances that still, after
fifty years, cry aloud for redress. The poem is "The
Assistant Draper's Petition," and the prodigal flow
of wit and fancy that marks it, so far from be-littling
its purpose, is surely fraught with a rare pathos,—
though the point of the jests is chiefly got from the
double meanings in well-known trade phrases:—

> Ah! who can tell the miseries of men
>   That serve the very cheapest shops in town?
> Till faint and weary, they leave off at ten,
>   Knock'd up by ladies beating of 'em down!

(Sydney Smith laid it down as a rule that wit and
pathos cannot dwell together,—that one must needs kill
the other; but he wrote his famous lecture without
knowing Thomas Hood.) And then there follows a
plea for leisure—leisure to read and to think,—the
leisure which noble Institutions like Toynbee Hall
are doing so much to foster and improve:

> O come then, gentle ladies, come in time,
>   O'erwhelm our counters, and unload our shelves;

Torment us all until the seventh chime,
But let us have the remnant to ourselves.'

We wish of knowledge to lay in a stock,
And not remain in ignorance incurable;—
To study Shakespeare, Milton, Dryden, Locke,
And other fabrics that have proved so durable.

We long for thoughts of intellectual kind,
And not to go bewilder'd to our beds;
With stuff and fustian taking up the mind,
And pins and needles running in our heads!

For oh! the brain gets very dull and dry,
Selling from morn till night for cash or credit:
Or with a vacant face and vacant eye,
Watching cheap prints that Knight did never edit.

Till sick with toil, and lassitude extreme,
We often think, when we are dull and vapoury,
The bliss of Paradise was so supreme,
Because that Adam did not deal in drapery'.

It would be absurd to pretend that Hood's lighter
verse is always up to the same level. It was his mis-
fortune to have to write for bread, and to struggle for
half a lifetime against poverty and ill-health. Much
of his "comic copy" was manufactured, and that too
when he was gravely ill, sitting propped up with
pillows. The marvel is not that the quality was often
so poor, but that he wrote so much that will live.
He was only forty-five when he died, and for the last

twenty years had dwelt " in company with pain." We probably owe to this circumstance that not only in his serious poetry, his " Bridge of Sighs," " Song of the Shirt," the " Haunted House," and the "Elm Tree," but also in his humorous verse, his fancy turned so habitually to some or other form of death or suffering. A glance at the titles in our index will show how often he found suggestions of humour in " violent ends," in accident and disaster.   In the serious poems, indeed, a different origin may be found for this.   Hood's own deep compassion and his sense of man's inhumanity was, doubtless, quickened by his own experience of pain and disappointment, and by the shadow of decay and doom that never lifted.   But he made no boast of it, or capital out of it ; the pessimistic accent is never heard in his verse ; he never lost his own cheerful faith in providence, though he early learned that

> There's not a string attuned to mirth,
> But has its chord in Melancholy.

And the treatment of " catastrophe " in his lighter verse is too purely fantastic to be even grim, still less to leave any ill flavour of bad taste.   He could never overlook the humorous analogies of things, even when they were his own sufferings.   " I am obliged to lead a very sedentary life," he wrote to a correspondent—" in fact, to be very chair-y of myself." And when for his poor wasted frame, his faithful wife was preparing a mustard plaster, he murmured, " Ah ! Jane—a great deal of mustard to a very little meat ! "

What has been said of Hood's punning faculty applies to the general quality of his humorous verse, namely, that the writer comes to it from a higher ground. Owing to ill-health he had been from childhood an omnivorous reader, but his sympathies were with all that is best in literature. He had trained himself on the best poetic models. Shakespeare and Keats were the inspiration of his earliest verse ; and often in the hastiest of comic effusions the eye and practised hand of the poet are discernible. Just as he did not hesitate to let a pun heighten the effect of some poignant reflection, as in the "Ode to Melancholy,"—

> Even the bright extremes of joy
> Bring on conclusions of disgust,
> Like the sweet blossoms of the May
> Whose fragrance ends in must,—

so he did not grudge a really noble fancy even to some perfunctory copy for a magazine, where the first aim was to raise a laugh. There is a poem of his about *a somnambulist (suggested by a once popular story,* Edgar Huntly), *the point of which is the contrast of the sleeper's romantic dream with the hard reality of the kitchen stairs down which he falls. The dreamer imagines himself in the rapids above Niagara, and as he nears the brink, he notices the rainbow hovering in the spray below, and feels that the old pledge and covenant of Hope is, in his case, the emblem of despair, —a thought that might have made the fortune of a sonnet or other lyric, had its author reserved it,—but he leaves it there. And this habit makes it difficult to classify his verse, the serious poetry often adopting the humorist's methods and the humorous often containing elements of genuine poetry. The present selection, while excluding the former of these, succeeds, I think, in showing Hood's versatility and ingenuity in the latter. The " Demon Ship " exhibits the same hand that depicted the anguish of Eugene Aram : the " Mermaid of Margate " is a playful parody of the Romantic legend of Bürger and his English followers ; while others, such as " Sally Brown " and " Nelly Gray," show the humorous possi- bilities of the Percy Ballad. The " Epping Hunt " is undisguisedly suggested by " John Gilpin," a*

"*Death's Ramble*" *is by the* "*Devil's Walk*" *of Coleridge and Southey—and* "*Queen Mab*" *shows how well Hood might have written for children, had he chosen to work the vein, in the delightful fashion of Mr. R. L. Stevenson.*

True poet and true humorist, Hood doubtless produced too much in both kinds for his fame. Struggling against "*two weak evils*," *poverty and disease, he too often wrote when the fountains of his fancy were dry. But if he diluted his reputation in some ways, he was growing and* "*making himself*" *in others more important. He was a learner to the end—widening as well as deepening in his human insight, recognising, as he told Sir Robert Peel in his last pathetic letter, the dangers of a* "*one-sided humanity, opposite to that Catholic Shakespearian sympathy, which felt with king as well as peasant, and duly estimated the mortal temptations of both stations.*" *Hood's position among our minor poets is peculiar and interesting. He is much loved, but not much written about. Critics will seldom be found analysing and dissecting his* "*work.*" *The scholar and the artist, the classic and the student of form, have their just and necessary place in our*

*literature, and they will not grudge Hood that certain
immortality which he won by paths so different. The
large-hearted Landor was certainly not wanting in
the qualities which he confessed his despair of
attaining in presence of such a writer as this, and
yet he clearly felt the difference between his own
power, and that which is destined to survive in the
"general heart of men," when he wrote—*

> *Jealous, I own it, I was once,*
> *That wickedness I here renounce.*
> *I tried at wit, it would not do;*
> *At tenderness, that failed me too;*
> *Before me on each path there stood*
> *The witty and the tender Hood.*

A. A.

Haseley Manor, Oxon.
    Oct. 1893.

CONTENTS

STRIDING in the Steps of Strutt—the historian of the old English Sports—the author of the following pages has endeavoured to record a yearly revel, already fast hastening to decay. The Easter Chase will soon be numbered with the pastimes of past times : its dogs will have had their day, and its Deer will be Fallow. A few more seasons, and this City Common Hunt will become uncommon.

In proof of this melancholy decadence, the ensuing epistle is inserted. It was penned by an underling at the Wells, a person more accustomed to riding than writing :—

" Sir,—About the Hunt. In anser to your Innqueries, their as been a great falling off laterally, so much so this year that there was nobody allmost. We did a mear nothing provisionally,

B

hardly a Bottle extra, wich is a proof in Pint.   In short our
Hunt may be said to be in the last Stag of a decline.

"I am, Sir,

"With respects from your humble Servant,

"BARTHOLOMEW RUTT."

"On Monday they began to hunt."—*Chevy Chase.*

OHN HUGGINS was as bold a man
        As trade did ever know,
    A warehouse good he had, that stood
        Hard by the church of Bow.

There people bought Dutch cheeses round,
    And single Glo'ster flat,—
And English butter in a lump,
    And Irish—in a *pat.*

Six days a week beheld him stand,
    His business next his heart,
At *counter*, with his apron tied
    About his *counter-part.*

The seventh in a Sluice-house box,
    He took his pipe and pot;

On Sundays for *eel-piety*,
A very noted spot.

'*At counter.*'

Ah, blest if he had never gone
Beyond its rural shed !
One Easter-tide, some evil guide
Put Epping in his head ;

Epping for butter justly famed,
And pork in sausage popp'd ;
Where winter time, or summer time,
Pig's flesh is always *chopt*.

But famous more, as annals tell,
    Because of Easter Chase :
There ev'ry year, 'twixt dog and deer,
    There is a gallant race.

With Monday's sun John Huggins rose,
    And slapt his leather thigh,
And sang the burthen of the song,
    " This day a stag must die."

For all the livelong day before,
    And all the night in bed,
Like Beckford, he had nourished " Thoughts
    On Hunting " in his head.

Of horn and morn, and hark and bark,
    And echo's answering sounds,
All poets' wit hath ever writ
    In *dog*-rel verse of *hounds*.

Alas ! there was no warning voice
    To whisper in his ear,
Thou art a fool in leaving *Cheap*
    To go and hunt the *deer !*

No thought he had of twisted spine,
   Or broken arms or legs ;
Not *chicken-hearted* he, altho'
   'Twas whispered of his *eggs !*

'*Of lustre superfine.*'

Ride out he would, and hunt he would,
   Nor dreamt of ending ill ; ·
Mayhap with Dr. *Ridout's* fee,   .
   And Surgeon *Hunter's* bill.

So he drew on his Sunday boots,
   Of lustre superfine ;
The liquid black they wore that day,
   Was *Warren*-ted to shine.

His yellow buckskins fitted close,
   As once upon a stag ;
Thus well equipt he gaily skipt,
   At once, upon his nag.

But first to him that held the rein,
   A crown he nimbly flung :
For holding of the horse ?—why, no—
   For holding of his tongue.

To say the horse was Huggins' own,
   Would only be a brag ;
His neighbour Fig and he went halves,
   Like Centaurs, in a nag.

And he that day had got the grey,
   Unknown to brother cit ;
The horse he knew would never tell,
   Altho' it was a *tit*.

A well-bred horse he was, I wis,
As he began to show,
By quickly " rearing up within
The way he ought to go."

' As he began to show.'

But Huggins, like a wary man,
Was ne'er from saddle cast ;
Resolved, by going very slow,
On sitting very fast.

And so he jogged to Tot'n'am Cross,
    An ancient town well known,
Where Edward wept for Eleanor
    In mortar and in stone.

A royal game of fox and goose,
    To play on such a loss ;
Wherever she set down her *orts*,
    Thereby he put a *cross*.

Now Huggins had a crony here,
    That lived beside the way ;
One that had promised sure to be
    His comrade for the day.

Whereas the man had changed his mind,
    Meanwhile upon the case !
And meaning not to hunt at all,
    Had gone to Enfield Chase.

For why, his spouse had made him vow
    To let a game alone,
Where folks that ride a bit of blood,
    May break a bit of bone.

" Now, be his wife a plague for life !
 A coward sure is he : "
Then Huggins turned his horse's head,
 And crossed the bridge of Lea.

'His spouse had made him vow.

Thence slowly on thro' Laytonstone,
 Past many a Quaker's box,—
No friends to hunters after deer,
 Tho' followers of a *Fox.*

And many a score behind—before—
    The self-same route inclined,
And minded all to march one way,
    Made one great march of mind.

Gentle and simple, he and she,
    And swell, and blood, and prig ;
And some had carts, and some a chaise,
    According to their gig.

Some long-eared jacks, some knacker's hacks
    (However odd it sounds),
Let out that day *to hunt*, instead
    Of going to the hounds !

And some had horses of their own,
    And some were forced to job it :
And some, while they inclined to *Hunt*,
    Betook themselves to *Cob-it*.

All sorts of vehicles and vans,
    Bad, middling, and the smart ;
Here rolled along the gay barouche,
    And there a dirty cart !

And lo ! a cart that held a squad
Of costermonger line ;
With one poor hack, like Pegasus,
That slaved for all the Nine !

'" Hallo !" cried they ; " come, trot away.
Copyright 1893 by Macmillan & Co.

Yet marvel not at any load,
That any horse might drag,
When all, that morn, at once were drawn
Together by a stag !

Now when they saw John Huggins go
   At such a sober pace ;
" Hallo ! " cried they ; " come, trot away,
   You'll never see the chase ! "

But John, as grave as any judge,
   Made answer quite as blunt ;
" It will be time enough to trot,
   When I begin to hunt ! "

And so he paced to Woodford Wells,
   Where many a horseman met,
And letting go the *reins*, of course,
   Prepared for *heavy wet*.

And lo ! within the crowded door,
   Stood Rounding, jovial elf ;
Here shall the Muse frame no excuse,
   But frame the man himself.

A snow-white head, a merry eye,
   A cheek of jolly blush ;
A claret tint laid on by health,
   With Master Reynard's brush ;

A hearty frame, a courteous bow,
  The prince he learned it from ;
His age about threescore and ten,
  And there you have Old Tom.

In merriest key I trow was he,
  So many guests to boast ;
So certain congregations meet,
  And elevate the host.

" Now welcome, lads," quoth he, " and prads,
  You're all in glorious luck :
Old Robin has a run to-day,
  A noted forest buck.

" Fair Mead's the place, where Bob and Tom,
  In red already ride ;
'Tis but a *step*, and on a horse
  You soon may go a *stride*."

So off they scampered, man and horse,
  As time and temper pressed—
But Huggins, hitching on a tree,
  Branched off from all the rest.

Howbeit he tumbled down in time
To join with Tom and Bob,
All in Fair Mead, which held that day
Its own fair meed of mob.

'" Now welcome, lads," quoth he.'

Idlers to wit—no Guardians some,
Of Tattlers in a squeeze ;
Ramblers, in heavy carts and vans,
Spectators, up in trees.

Butchers on backs of butchers' hacks,
  That shambled to and fro !
Bakers intent upon a buck,
  Neglectful of the *dough !*

Change Alley Bears to speculate,
  As usual, for a fall ;
And green and scarlet runners, such
  As never climbed a wall !

'Twas strange to think what difference
  A single creature made ;
A single stag had caused a whole
  *Stag*nation in their trade.

Now Huggins from his saddle rose,
  And in the stirrups stood :
And lo ! a little cart that came
  Hard by a little wood.

In shape like half a hearse,—tho' not
  For corpses in the least ;
For this contained the *deer alive,*
  And not the *dear deceased !*

And now began a sudden stir,
    And then a sudden shout,
The prison-doors were opened wide,
    And Robin bounded out !

His antlered head shone blue and red,
    Bedecked with ribbons fine ;
Like other bucks that come to 'list
    The hawbucks in the line.

One curious gaze of mild amaze,
    He turned and shortly took ;
Then gently ran adown the mead,
    And bounded o'er the brook.

Now Huggins, standing far aloof,
    Had never seen the deer,
Till all at once he saw the beast
    Come charging in his rear.

Away he went, and many a score
    Of riders did the same,
On horse and ass—like High and Low
    And Jack pursuing Game !

Good Lord ! to see the riders now,
   Thrown off with sudden whirl,
A score within the purling brook,
   Enjoyed their " early purl."

' *Enjoyed their " early purl."* '

A score were sprawling on the grass,
   And beavers fell in showers ;
There was another *Floorer* there,
   Beside the Queen of Flowers !

Some lost their stirrups, some their whips,
   Some had no caps to show ;

C

But few, like Charles at Charing Cross,
   Rode on in *Statue* quo.

"O dear! O dear!" now might you hear,
   "I've surely broke a bone;"
"My head is sore,"—with many more
   Such speeches from the *thrown*.

Howbeit their wailings never moved
   The wide Satanic clan,
Who grinned, as once the Devil grinned,
   To see the fall of Man.

And hunters good, that understood,
   Their laughter knew no bounds,
To see the horses "throwing off,"
   So long before the hounds.

For deer must have due course of law,
   Like men the Courts among;
Before those Barristers the dogs
   Proceed to "giving tongue."

And now Old Robin's foes were set,
　That fatal taint to find,
That always is scent after him,
　Yet always left behind.

And here observe how dog and man
　A different temper shows,
What hound resents that he is sent
　To follow his own nose ?

Towler and Jowler—howlers all,
　No single tongue was mute ;
The stag had led a hart, and lo !
　The whole pack followed suit.

No spur he lacked ; fear stuck a knife
　And fork in either haunch ;
And every dog he knew had got
　An eye-tooth to his paunch !

Away, away ! he scudded like
　A ship before the gale ;
Now flew to " hills we know not of,"
　Now, nun-like, took the vale.

Another squadron charging now,
Went off at furious pitch ;—
A perfect Tam o' Shanter mob,
Without a single witch.

But who was he with flying skirts,
A hunter did endorse,
And like a poet seemed to ride
Upon a wingèd horse,—

A whipper-in ?—no whipper-in :
A huntsman ? no such soul.
A connoisseur, or amateur ?
Why yes,—a Horse Patrol.

A member of police, for whom
The county found a nag,
And, like Acteon in the tale,
He found himself in stag !

Away they went then, dog and deer,
And hunters all away,—
The maddest horses never knew
Mad staggers such as they !

Some gave a shout, some rolled about,

And anticked as they rode,

And butchers whistled on their curs,

And milkmen *tally-hoed*.

' *Each thicket served to thin it.*'

About two score there were, not more,

That galloped in the race ;

The rest, alas ! lay on the grass,

As once in Chevy Chase !

But even those that galloped on
  Were fewer every minute,—
The field kept getting more select,
  Each thicket served to thin it.

For some pulled up, and left the hunt,
  Some fell in miry bogs,
And vainly rose and " ran a muck,"
  To overtake the dogs.

And some, in charging hurdle stakes,
  Were left bereft of sense—
What else could be premised of blades
  That never learned to fence ?

But Rounding, Tom, and Bob, no gate,
  Nor hedge, nor ditch, could stay ;
O'er all they went, and did the work
  Of leap years in a day.

And by their side see Huggins ride,
  As fast as he could speed ;
For, like Mazeppa, he was quite
  At mercy of his steed.

No means he had, by timely check,
    The gallop to remit,
For firm and fast, between his teeth,
    The biter held the bit.

Trees raced along, all Essex fled
    Beneath him as he sate,—
He never saw a county go
    At such a county rate !

" Hold hard ! hold hard ! you'll lame the dogs."
    Quoth Huggins, " So I do,—
I've got the saddle well in hand,
    And hold as hard as you ! "

Good Lord ! to see him ride along,
    And throw his arms about,
As if with stitches in the side,
    That he was drawing out !

And now he bounded up and down,
    Now like a jelly shook :
Till bumped and galled—yet not where Gall
    For bumps did ever look !

And rowing with his legs the while,
    As tars are apt to ride,
With every kick he gave a prick,
    Deep in the horse's side !

' And like a bird was singing out.'

But soon the horse was well avenged,
    For cruel smart of spurs,
For, riding through a moor, he pitched
    His master in a furze !

Where sharper set than hunger is
    He squatted all forlorn ;

And like a bird was singing out
 While sitting on a thorn !

Right glad was he, as well might be,
 Such cushion to resign :
" Possession is nine points," but his
 Seemed more than ninety-nine.

Yet worse than all the prickly points
 That entered in his skin,
His nag was running off the while
 The thorns were running in !

Now had a Papist seen his sport
 Thus laid upon the shelf,
Altho' no horse he had to cross,
 He might have crossed himself.

Yet surely still the wind is ill
 That none can say is fair ;
A jolly wight there was, that rode
 Upon a sorry mare !

A sorry mare, that surely came
　　Of pagan blood and bone ;
For down upon her knees she went
　　To many a stock and stone !

Now seeing Huggins' nag adrift,
　　This farmer, shrewd and sage,
Resolved, by changing horses here,
　　To hunt another stage !

Tho' felony, yet who would let
　　Another's horse alone,
Whose neck is placed in jeopardy
　　By riding on his own ?

And yet the conduct of the man
　　Seemed honest-like and fair ;
For he seemed willing, horse and all,
　　To go before the *mare !*

So up on Huggins' horse he got,
　　And swiftly rode away,
While Huggins mounted on the mare,
　　Done brown upon a bay !

And off they set, in double chase,
For such was fortune's whim,
The farmer rode to hunt the stag,
And Huggins hunted him !

' So up on Huggins' horse he got.'

Alas ! with one that rode so well
In vain it was to strive ;
A dab was he, as dabs should be—
All leaping and alive !

And here of Nature's kindly care
　　Behold a curious proof,
As nags are meant to leap, she puts
　　A frog in every hoof!

Whereas the mare, altho' her share
　　She had of hoof and frog,
On coming to a gate stopped short
　　As stiff as any log ;

Whilst Huggins in the stirrup stood
　　With neck like neck of crane,
As sings the Scottish song—" to see
　　The *gate* his *hart* had gane."

And lo ! the dim and distant hunt
　　Diminished in a trice :
The steeds, like Cinderella's team,
　　Seemed dwindling into mice ;

And, far remote, each scarlet coat
　　Soon flitted like a spark,—
Tho' still the forest murmured back
　　An echo of the bark !

But sad at soul John Huggins turned :

No comfort could he find ;

Whilst thus the " Hunting Chorus " sped,

To stay five bars behind.

' Whilst Huggins in the stirrup stood.'

For tho' by dint of spur he got

A leap in spite of fate—

Howbeit there was no toll at all,
　　They could not clear the gate.

And, like Fitzjames, he cursed the hunt, ·
　　And sorely cursed the day,
And mused a new Gray's elegy
　　On his departed grey!

Now many a sign at Woodford town
　　Its Inn-vitation tells :
But Huggins, full of ills, of course,
　　Betook him to the Wells.

Where Rounding tried to cheer him up
　　With many a merry laugh ;
But Huggins thought of neighbour Fig,
　　And called for half-and-half.

Yet, 'spite of drink, he could not blink
　　Remembrance of his loss ;
To drown a care like his, required
　　Enough to drown a horse.

When thus forlorn, a merry horn
Struck up without the door,—
The mounted mob were all returned ;
The Epping Hunt was o'er !

"Beasts of draught!"

And many a horse was taken out
Of saddle and of shaft ;
And men, by dint of drink, became
The only *" beasts of draught ! "*

For now begun a harder run
    On wine, and gin, and beer ;
And overtaken man discussed
    The overtaken deer.

How far he ran, and eke how fast,
    And how at bay he stood,
Deer-like, resolved to sell his life
    As dearly as he could ;

And how the hunters stood aloof,
    Regardful of their lives,
And shunned a beast, whose very horns
    They knew could *handle* knives !

How Huggins stood when he was rubbed
    By help and ostler kind,
And when they cleaned the clay before,
    How worse " remained behind."

And one, how he had found a horse
    Adrift—a goodly grey !
And kindly rode the nag, for fear
    The nag should go astray.

'When he was rubbed.'
Copyright 1893 by Macmillan & Co.

D

Now Huggins, when he heard the tale,
　　Jumped up with sudden glee ;
" A goodly grey ! why, then, I say
　　That grey belongs to me !

" Let me endorse again my horse,
　　Delivered safe and sound ;　　·
And, gladly, I will give the man
　　A bottle and a pound ! "

The wine was drunk,—the money paid,
　　Tho' not without remorse,
To pay another man so much,
　　For riding on his horse.

And let the chase again take place,
　　For many a long, long year,
John Huggins will not ride again
　　To hunt the Epping Deer !

MORAL.

Thus pleasure oft eludes our grasp,
　　Just when we think to grip her ;
And hunting after happiness,
　　We only hunt a slipper.

ADVERTISEMENT TO THE SECOND EDITION OF
EPPING HUNT.

The Publisher begs leave to say that he has had the following letter from the Author of this little book :—

" Dear Sir,—I am much gratified to learn from you, that the Epping Hunt has had *such a run* that it is *quite exhausted*, and that you intend, therefore, to give the work what may be called ' *second wind*,' by a new impression.

" I attended the last Anniversary of the Festival, and am concerned to say that the sport does not improve, but appears an ebbing as well as Epping custom. The run was miserable indeed ; but what was to be expected ? The chase was a Doe, and, consequently, the Hunt set off with the *Hind* part before. It was, therefore, quite in character for so many Nimrods to start, as they did, before the hounds, but which, as you know, is quite contrary to the *Lex Tallyho-nis*, or Laws of Hunting.

" I dined with the Master of the Revel, who is as hale as ever, and promises to reside some time in the *Wells* ere he *kicks the bucket*. He is an honest, hearty, worthy man, and when he dies there will be ' a cry of dogs ' in his kennel.

" I am, dear Sir, yours, &c.,

" T. HOOD.

" WINCHMORE HILL, *June* 1830."

FAITHLESS SALLY BROWN

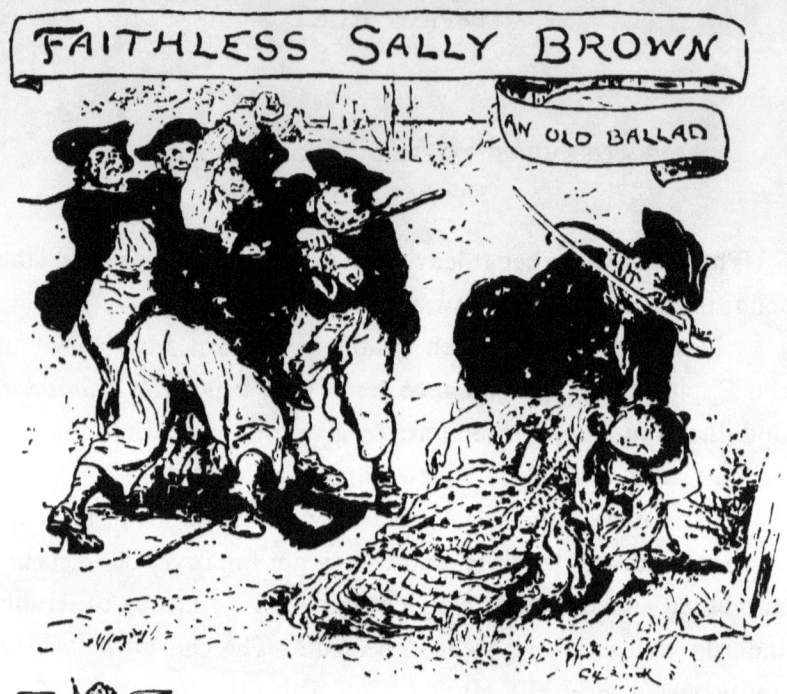

AN OLD BALLAD

YOUNG Ben he was a nice young man,
  A carpenter by trade;
And he fell in love with Sally Brown,
  That was a lady's maid.

But as they fetched a walk one day,
  They met a press-gang crew;
And Sally she did faint away,
  Whilst Ben he was brought to.

The Boatswain swore with wicked words,
    Enough to shock a saint,
That though she did seem in a fit,
    'Twas nothing but a feint.

" Come, girl," said he, " hold up your head,
    He'll be as good as me ;
For when your swain is in our boat,
    A boatswain he will be."

So when they'd made their game of her,
    And taken off her elf,
She roused, and found she only was
    A coming to herself.

" And is he gone, and is he gone ? "
    She cried, and wept outright :
" Then I will to the water side,
    And see him out of sight."

A waterman came up to her,
    " Now, young woman," said he,
" If you weep on so, you will make
    Eye-water in the sea."

" Alas ! they've taken my beau Ben

To sail with old Benbow ; "

And her woe began to run afresh,

As if she'd said Gee woe !

'" Now, young woman," said he.'
Copyright 1893 by Macmillan & Co.

Says he, " They've only taken him

To the Tender ship, you see ; "

" The Tender ship," cried Sally Brown,

" What a hard-ship that must be !

"Oh! would I were a mermaid now,
  For then I'd follow him ;
But oh ! I'm not a fish-woman,
  And so I cannot swim.

"Alas! I was not born beneath
  The Virgin and the Scales,
So I must curse my cruel stars,
  And walk about in Wales."

Now Ben had sailed to many a place
  That's underneath the world ;
But in two years the ship came home,
  And all her sails were furled.

But when he called on Sally Brown,
  To see how she went on,
He found she'd got another Ben,
  Whose Christian name was John.

"O Sally Brown, O Sally Brown !
  How could you serve me so ?
I've met with many a breeze before,
  But never such a blow."

Then reading on his 'bacco box,

He heaved a bitter sigh,

And then began to eye his pipe,

And then to pipe his eye.

'He found she'd got another Ben.'
Copyright 1893 by Macmillan & Co.

And then he tried to sing "All's Well,"

But could not though he tried :

His head was turned, and so he chewed
  His pigtail till he died.

His death, which happened in his berth,
  At forty-odd befell :
They went and told the sexton, and
  The sexton toll'd the bell.

THE MERMAID OF MARGATE.

" Alas ! what perils do environ
That man who meddles with a siren ! "

Hudibras.

On Margate Beach, where the sick one roams,
  And the sentimental reads ;
Where the maiden flirts, and the widow comes
  Like the ocean—to cast her weeds ;—

Where urchins wander to pick up shells,
  And the Cit to spy at the ships,—
Like the water gala at Sadler's Wells,—
  And the Chandler for watery dips ;—

There's a maiden sits by the ocean brim,
  As lovely and fair as sin !
But woe, deep water and woe to him,
  That she snareth like Peter Fin !

Her head is crowned with pretty sea-wares,
  And her locks are golden and loose,
And seek to her feet, like other folks' heirs,
  To stand, of course, in her shoes !

And all day long she combeth them well,
  With a sea-shark's prickly jaw ;
And her mouth is just like a rose-lipped shell,
  The fairest that man e'er saw !

And the Fishmonger, humble as love may be,
  Hath planted his seat by her side ;
" Good even, fair maid !   Is thy lover at sea,
  To make thee so watch the tide ? "

She turned about with her pearly brows,
  And clasped him by the hand ;
" Come, love, with me ; I've a bonny house
  On the golden Goodwin sand."

And then she gave him a siren kiss,
    No honeycomb e'er was sweeter ;
Poor wretch ! how little he dreamt for this
    That Peter should be salt-Peter :

'*And clasped him by the hand.*

And away with her prize to the wave she leapt,
    Not walking, as damsels do,
With toe and heel, as she ought to have stept,
    But she hopt like a Kangaroo ;

One plunge, and then the victim was blind,
   Whilst they galloped across the tide ;
At last, on the bank he waked in his mind,
   And the Beauty was by his side.

' *His hair began to stiffen.*'

One half on the sand, and half in the sea,
   But his hair began to stiffen ;
For when he looked where her feet should be,
   She had no more feet than Miss Biffen !

But a scaly tail, of a dolphin's growth,
   In the dabbling brine did soak :

At last she opened her pearly mouth,
  Like an oyster, and thus she spoke :

" You crimpt my father, who was a skate,- -
  And my sister you sold—a maid ;
So here remain for a fish'ry fate,
  For lost you are, and betrayed ! "

And away she went, with a sea-gull's scream,
  And a splash of her saucy tail ;
In a moment he lost the silvery gleam
  That shone on her splendid mail !

The sun went down with a blood-red flame,
  And the sky grew cloudy and black,
And the tumbling billows like leap-frog came,
  Each over the other's back !

Ah me ! it had been a beautiful scene,
  With the safe terra-firma round ;
But the green water-hillocks all seem'd to him,
  Like those in a churchyard ground ;

And Christians love in the turf to lie,
  Not in watery graves to be ;
Nay, the very fishes will sooner die
  On the land than in the sea.

And whilst he stood, the watery strife
  Encroached on every hand,
And the ground decreased—his moments of life
  Seemed measured, like Time's, by sand ;

And still the waters foamed in, like ale,
  In front, and on either flank,
He knew that Goodwin and Co. must fail,
  There was such a run on the bank.

A little more, and a little more,
  The surges came tumbling in,
He sang the evening hymn twice o'er,
  And thought of every sin !

Each flounder and plaice lay cold at his heart,
  As cold as his marble slab ;
And he thought he felt, in every part,
  The pincers of scalded crab.

The squealing lobsters that he had boiled,
　　And the little potted shrimps,
All the horny prawns he had ever spoiled,
　　Gnawed into his soul, like imps!

And the billows were wandering to and fro,
　　And the glorious sun was sunk,
And Day, getting black in the face, as though
　　Of the night-shade she had drunk!

Had there been but a smuggler's cargo adrift,
　　One tub, or keg, to be seen,
It might have given his spirits a lift
　　Or an *anker* where *Hope* might lean!

But there was not a box or a beam afloat,
　　To raft him from that sad place;
Not a skiff, not a yawl, or a mackerel boat,
　　Nor a smack upon Neptune's face.

At last, his lingering hopes to buoy,
　　He saw a sail and a mast,
And called " Ahoy!"—but it was not a hoy,
　　And so the vessel went past.

And with saucy wing that flapped in his face,
　The wild bird about him flew,
With a shrilly scream, that twitted his case,
　" Why, thou art a sea-gull too ! "

' " Ahoy ! " '

And lo ! the tide was over his feet ;
　Oh ! his heart began to freeze,
And slowly to pulse :—in another beat
　The wave was up to his knees !

He was deafened amidst the mountain tops,
　And the salt spray blinded his eyes,

E

And washed away the other salt drops
    That grief had caused to arise :—

But just as his body was all afloat,
    And the surges above him broke,
He was saved from the hungry deep by a boat
    Of Deal—(but builded of oak).

The skipper gave him a dram, as he lay,
    And chafed his shivering skin ;
And the Angel returned that was flying away
    With the spirit of Peter Fin.

ON Hounslow Heath—and close beside the
road,
As western travellers may oft have seen,—
A little house some years ago there stood,
A minikin abode ;
And built like Mr. Birkbeck's, all of wood :
The walls of white, the window-shutters green,—
Four wheels it had at North, South, East, and West
(Though now at rest),
On which it used to wander to and fro,
Because its master ne'er maintained a rider,
Like those who trade in Paternoster Row ;

But made his business travel for itself,
         Till he had made his pelf,
And then retired—if one may call it so,
         Of a roadsider.

Perchance, the very race and constant riot
Of stages, long and short, which thereby ran,
Made him more relish the repose and quiet
         Of his now sedentary caravan ;
Perchance, he loved the ground because 'twas common,
         And so he might impale a strip of soil
         That furnished, by his toil,
Some dusty greens, for him and his old woman ;—
And five tall hollyhocks, in dingy flower :
Howbeit, the thoroughfare did no ways spoil
His peace, unless, in some unlucky hour,
A stray horse came, and gobbled up his bow'r.

But tired of always looking at the coaches,
The same to come,—when they had seen them one
         day !
         And, used to brisker life, both man and wife
Began to suffer N U E's approaches,
And feel retirement like a long wet Sunday,—

So, having had some quarters of school breeding,

They turned themselves, like other folks, to reading ;

But setting out where others nigh have done,

And being ripened in the seventh stage,

The childhood of old age,

Began, as other children have begun,—

Not with the pastorals of Mr. Pope,

Or Bard of Hope,

Or Paley ethical, or learned Porson,

But spelt, on Sabbaths, in St. Mark, or John,

And then relax'd themselves with Whittington,

Or Valentine and Orson—

But chiefly fairy tales they loved to con,

And being easily melted in their dotage,

Slobber'd,—and kept

Reading,—and wept

Over the White Cat, in their wooden cottage,

Thus reading on—the longer

They read, of course, their childish faith grew stronger

In Gnomes, and Hags, and Elves, and Giants grim,—

If talking Trees and Birds revealed to him,

She saw the flight of Fairyland's fly-waggons,

And magic fishes swim

In puddle ponds, and took old crows for dragons,—

Both were quite drunk from the enchanted flagons;
When as it fell upon a summer's day,

'Reading.—and wept.

As the old man sat a feeding
On the old-babe reading,
Beside his open street-and-parlour door,
A hideous roar
Proclaimed a drove of beasts was coming by the way.

Long-horned, and short, of many a different breed,

Tall, tawny brutes, from famous Lincoln-levels

    Or Durham feed,

'A horn-pipe.'

With some of those unquiet black dwarf devils

    From nether side of Tweed,

    Or Firth of Forth ;

Looking half wild with joy to leave the North,—

With dusty hides, all mobbing on together,—

When,—whether from a fly's malicious comment
Upon his tender flank, from which he shrank ;
   Or whether
Only in some enthusiastic moment,—
However, one brown monster, in a frisk,
Giving his tail a perpendicular whisk,
Kicked out a passage through the beastly rabble ;
And after a pas seul,—or, if you will, a
Horn-pipe before the basket-maker's villa,
   Leapt o'er the tiny pale,—
Backed his beefsteaks against the wooden gable,
And thrust his brawny bell-rope of a tail
   Right o'er the page,
   Wherein the sage
Just then was spelling some romantic fable.

The old man, half a scholar, half a dunce,
Could not peruse,—who could ?—two tales at once ;
   And being huffed
At what he knew was none of Riquet's Tuft,
   Banged-to the door,
But most unluckily enclosed a morsel
Of the intruding tail, and all the tassel :—
   The monster gave a roar,

And bolting off with speed increased by pain,
The little house became a coach once more,
And, like Macheath, "took to the road" again !

'" Took to the road" again !'

Just then, by fortune's whimsical decree,
The ancient woman stooping with her crupper
Towards sweet home, or where sweet home should be,
Was getting up some household herbs for supper ;
Thoughtful of Cinderella, in the tale,
And, quaintly wondering if magic shifts

Could o'er a common pumpkin so prevail,
To turn it to a coach ;—what pretty gifts
Might come of cabbages, and curly kale ;

Meanwhile she never heard her old man's wail,
Nor turned, till home had turned a corner, quite
      Gone out of sight !

At last, conceive her, rising from the ground,
Weary of sitting on her russet clothing,

And looking round

Where rest was to be found,

There was no house—no villa there—no nothing!

No house!

The change was quite amazing ;

It made her senses stagger for a minute,

The riddle's explication seemed to harden ; ·

But soon her superannuated *nous*

Explain'd the horrid mystery ;—and raising

Her hand to heaven, with the cabbage in it,

On which she meant to sup,—

" Well ! this *is* Fairy Work !   I'll bet a farden,

Little Prince Silverwings has ketch'd me up,

And set me down in some one else's garden ! "

EQUESTRIAN COURTSHIP

t was a young maiden went forth to ride,
And there was a wooer to pace by her side;
His horse was so little, and hers so high,
He thought his angel was up in the sky.

His love was great, though his wit was small;
He bade her ride easy—and that was all.
The very horses began to neigh,—
Because their betters had nought to say.

They rode by elm, and they rode by oak,
They rode by a churchyard, and then he spoke:

" My pretty maiden, if you'll agree,
You shall always amble through life with me."

'*They rode by a churchyard, and then he spoke.*'
Copyright 1893 by Macmillan & Co.

The damsel answered him never a word,
But kicked the grey mare, and away she spurred.

The wooer still followed behind the jade,
And enjoyed—like a wooer—the dust she made.

They rode thro' moss, and they rode thro' moor,—
The gallant behind and the lass before :—
At last they came to a miry place,
And there the sad wooer gave up the chase.

Quoth he, " If my nag was better to ride,
I'd follow her over the world so wide.
Oh, it is not my love that begins to fail,
But I've lost the last glimpse of the grey mare's tail ! "

TIM TURPIN

A PATHETIC BALLAD

I.

Tim TURPIN he was gravel blind,
    And ne'er had seen the skies;
For Nature when his head was made,
    Forgot to dot his eyes.

II.

So, like a Christmas pedagogue,
    Poor Tim was forced to do—
Look out for pupils; for he had
    A vacancy for two.

III.

There's some have specs to help their sight
    Of objects dim and small:

But Tim had *specks* within his eyes,
And could not see at all.

'*Now Tim he wooed a servant maid.*'

IV.

Now Tim he wooed a servant maid,
And took her to his arms ;
For he, like Pyramus, had cast
A wall-eye on her charms.

V.

By day she led him up and down,
    Where'er he wished to jog,
A happy wife, altho' she led
    The life of any dog.

VI.

But just when Tim had lived a month
    In honey with his wife,
A surgeon op'd his Milton eyes,
    Like oysters, with a knife.

VII.

But when his eyes were opened thus,
    He wished them dark again :
For when he look'd upon his wife,
    He saw her very plain.

VIII.

Her face was bad, her figure worse,
    He couldn't bear to eat :
For she was anything but like
    A grace before his meat.

F

IX.

Now Tim he was a feeling man ;
For when his sight was thick
It made him feel for everything—
But that was with a stick.

'He saw her very plain.'

X.

So, with a cudgel in his hand—
It was not light or slim—
He knocked at his wife's head until
It opened unto him.

XI.

And when the corpse was stiff and cold,
  He took his slaughtered spouse,
And laid her in a heap with all
  The ashes of her house.

XII.

But like a wicked murderer,
  He lived in constant fear
From day to day, and so he cut
  His throat from ear to ear.

XIII.

The neighbours fetched a doctor in ;
  Said he, " This wound I dread
Can hardly be sewed up—his life
  Is hanging on a thread."

XIV.

But when another week was gone,
  He gave him stronger hope—
Instead of hanging on a thread,
  Of hanging on a rope.

XV.

Ah! when he hid his bloody work
In ashes round about,
How little he supposed the truth
Would soon be sifted out.

'A dozen men to try the fact.

XVI.

But when the parish dustman came,
His rubbish to withdraw,
He found more dust within the heap
Than he contracted for!

XVII.

A dozen men to try the fact
Were sworn that very day;

But though they all were jurors, yet
No conjurors were they.

XVIII.

Said Tim unto those jurymen,
You need not waste your breath,
For I confess myself at once
The author of her death.

XIX.

And, oh! when I reflect upon
The blood that I have spilt,
Just like a button is my soul,
Inscribed with double *guilt* !

XX.

Then turning round his head again,
He saw before his eyes,
A great judge, and a little judge,
The judges of a-size !

XXI.

The great judge took his judgment cap,
And put it on his head,

And sentenced Tim by law to hang
Till he was three times dead.

' A great judge, and a little judge.

XXII.

So he was tried, and he was hung
(Fit punishment for such)
On Horsham-drop, and none can say
It was a drop too much.

ONE day the dreary old King of Death
    Inclined for some sport with the carnal,
So he tied a pack of darts on his back,
    And quietly stole from his charnel.

His head was bald of flesh and of hair,
    His body was lean and lank,
His joints at each stir made a crack, and the cur
    Took a gnaw, by the way, at his shank.

And what did he do with his deadly darts,
    This goblin of grisly bone ?
He dabbled and spilled man's blood, and he killed
    Like a butcher that kills his own.

The first he slaughtered it made him laugh
   (For the man was a coffin-maker),
To think how the mutes, and men in black suits,
   Would mourn for an undertaker.

Death saw two Quakers sitting at church,
   Quoth he, " We shall not differ."
And he let them alone, like figures of stone,
   For he could not make them stiffer.

He saw two duellists going to fight,
   In fear they could not smother ;
And he shot one through at once—for he knew
   They never would shoot each other.

He saw a watchman fast in his box,
   And he gave a snore infernal ;
Said Death, " He may keep his breath, for his
     sleep
   Can never be more eternal."

He met a coachman driving his coach,
   So slow, that his fare grew sick ;

But he let him stray on his tedious way,
For Death only wars on the *quick*.

Death saw a toll-man taking a toll,
In the spirit of his fraternity ;

'*He saw a watchman fast in his box.*

But he knew that sort of man would extort
Though summoned to all eternity.

He found an author writing his life,
But he let him write no further ;
For Death, who strikes whenever he likes,
Is jealous of all self-murther !

Death saw a patient that pulled out his purse,
    And a doctor that took the sum ;
But he let them be—for he knew that the " fee "
    Was a prelude to " saw " and " sum."

' A patient that pulled out his purse.

He met a dustman ringing a bell,
    And he gave him a mortal thrust ;
For himself, by law, since Adam's flaw,
    Is contractor for all our dust.

He saw a sailor mixing his grog,

And he marked him out for slaughter;

'He saw a sailor mixing his grog.'

For on water he scarcely had cared for Death,

And never on rum-and-water.

Death saw two players playing at cards,

But the game wasn't worth a dump,

For he quickly laid them flat with a spade,

To wait for the final trump!

"Sweet Memory, wafted by thy gentle gale,
Oft up the stream of time I turn my sail."

ROGERS.

I.

COME, my Crony, let's think upon far-away
days,

And lift up a little Oblivion's veil ;

Let's consider the past with a lingering gaze,

Like a peacock whose eyes are inclined to his tail.

II.

Ay, come, let us turn our attention behind,

Like those critics whose heads are so heavy, I fear,

That they cannot keep up with the march of the mind,

And so turn face about for reviewing the rear.

III.

Looking over Time's crupper and over his tail,
   Oh! what ages and pages there are to revise!
And as farther our back-searching glances prevail,
   Like the emmets, " how little we are in our eyes ! "

IV.

What a sweet pretty innocent, half a yard long,
   On a dimity lap of true nursery make !
I can fancy I hear the old lullaby song
   That was meant to compose me, but kept me awake.

V.

Methinks I still suffer the infantine throes,
   When my flesh was a cushion for any long pin—
Whilst they patted my body to comfort my woes,
   Oh! how little they dreamt they were driving them
     in !

VI.

Infant sorrows are strong—infant pleasures as weak—
   But no grief was allowed to indulge in its note ;
Did you ever attempt a small " bubble and squeak,"
   Thro' the Dalby's Carminative down in your throat?

VII.

Did you ever go up to the roof with a bounce?

Did you ever come down to the floor with the
same?

' To comfort my woes.'

Oh! I can't but agree with both ends, and pronounce
"Head or tails" with a child, an unpleasantish
game!

VIII.

Then an urchin—I see myself urchin, indeed,
　　With a smooth Sunday face for a mother's delight ;
Why should weeks have an end ?—I am sure there
　　　　was need
　　Of a Sabbath to follow each Saturday night.

IX.

Was your face ever sent to the housemaid to scrub ?
　　Have you ever felt huckaback softened with sand ?
Had you ever your nose towelled up to a snub,
　　And your eyes knuckled out with the back of the
　　　　hand ?

X.

Then a schoolboy—my tailor was nothing in fault,
　　For an urchin will grow to a lad by degrees,—
But how well I remember that " pepper and salt "
　　That was down to the elbows, and up to the knees !

XI.

What a figure it cut when as Norval I spoke !
　　With a lanky right leg duly planted before ;

Whilst I told of the chief that was killed by my stroke,

And extended *my* arms as "the arms that he wore!"

' Was your face ever sent to the housemaid to scrub ?'

XII.

Next a Lover—Oh! say, were you ever in love?

With a lady too cold—and your bosom too hot!

Have you bowed to a shoe-tie, and knelt to a glove,

Like a *beau* that desired to be tied in a knot?

G

XIII.

With the bride all in white, and your body in blue,
  Did you walk up the aisle—the genteelest of men ?
When I think of that beautiful vision anew,
  Oh ! I seem but the *biffin* of what I was then !

XIV.

I am withered and worn by a premature care,
  And my wrinkles confess the decline of my days ;
Old Time's busy hand has made free with my hair,
  And I'm seeking to hide it—by writing for bays.

HERE'S some is born with their legs
straight by natur—
And some is born with bow-legs from the
first—
And some that should have growed a good deal
straighter,
But they were badly nursed,
And set, you see, like Bacchus, with their pegs
Astride of casks and kegs.
I've got myself a sort of bow to larboard,
And starboard,
And this is what it was that warped my legs :

'Twas all along of Poll, as I may say,

That foul'd my cable when I ought to slip ;

But on the tenth of May,

When I gets under weigh,

"'Twas all along of Poll.'

Copyright 1893 by Macmillan & Co.

Down there in Hartfordshire, to join my ship,

I sees the mail

Get under sail,

The only one there was to make the trip.

Well, I gives chase,
But as she run
Two knots to one,
There warn't no use in keeping on the race !

Well, casting round about, what next to try on,
And how to spin,
I spies an ensign with a Bloody Lion,
And bears away to leeward for the inn,
Beats round the gable,
And fetches up before the coach horse stable.
Well, there they stand, four kickers in a row,
And so
I just makes free to cut a brown 'un's cable.
But riding isn't in a seaman's natur ;
So I whips out a toughish end of yarn,
And gets a kind of sort of a land-waiter
To splice me, heel to heel,
Under the she-mare's keel,
And off I goes, and leaves the inn a-starn !

My eyes ! how she did pitch !
And wouldn't keep her own to go in no line,

Tho' I kept bowsing, bowsing at her bow-line,

But always making lee-way to the ditch,

'*To splice me, heel to heel.*'

And yawed her head about all sorts of ways.

The devil sink the craft!

And wasn't she tremendous slack in stays!

We couldn't, no how, keep the inn abaft!

Well, I suppose

We hadn't run a knot—or much beyond—
(What will you have on it ?)—but off she goes,
Up to her bends in a fresh-water pond !
> There I am ! all a-back !
So I looks forward for her bridle-gears,
To heave her head round on the t'other tack ;
> But when I starts,
> The leather parts,
And goes away right over by the ears !

.

> What could a fellow do,
Whose legs, like mine, you know, were in the bilboes,
But trim myself upright for bringing-to,
And square his yard-arms and brace up his elbows,
> In rig all snug and clever,
Just while his craft was taking in her water ?
I didn't like my berth, though, howsomdever,
Because the yarn, you see, kept getting tauter.
Says I—I wish this job was rayther shorter !

> The chase had gained a mile
Ahead, and still the she-mare stood a-drinking ;
> Now, all the while
Her body didn't take, of course, to shrinking.
Says I, she's letting out her reefs, I'm thinking ;

'My legs began to bend like winkin.'
Copyright 1893 by Macmillan & Co.

And so she swelled and swelled,

And yet the tackle held,

Till both my legs began to bend like winkin.

My eyes! but she took in enough to founder!

And there's my timbers straining every bit,

Ready to split,
And her tarnation hull a-growing rounder!

Well, there—off Hartford Ness
We lay both lashed and water-logged together,
And can't contrive a signal of distress.
Thinks I, we must ride out this here foul weather,
Tho' sick of riding out, and nothing less;
When, looking round, I sees a man a-starn:
"Hollo!" says I, "come underneath her quarter!"
And hands him out my knife to cut the yarn.
So I gets off, and lands upon the road,
And leaves the she-mare to her own consarn,
A-standing by the water.
If I get on another, I'll be blowed!
And that's the way, you see, my legs got bowed!

John Trot
A Ballad

I.

JOHN TROT he was as tall a lad
    As York did ever rear—
As his dear Granny used to say,
    He'd make a grenadier.

II.

A sergeant soon came down to York,
    With ribbons and a frill ;
My lads, said he, let broadcast be,
    And come away to drill.

III.

But when he wanted John to 'list,
  In war he saw no fun,
Where what is called a raw recruit
  Gets often over-done.

IV.

Let others carry guns, said he,
  And go to war's alarms,
But I have got a shoulder-knot
  Imposed upon my arms.

V.

For John he had a footman's place
  To wait on Lady Wye—
She was a dumpy woman, tho'
  Her family was high.

VI.

Now when two years had passed away,
  Her lord took very ill,
And left her to her widowhood,
  Of course more dumpy still.

VII.

Said John, I am a proper man,
　　And very tall to see ;
Who knows, but now her lord is low,
　　She may look up to me ?

VIII.

A cunning woman told me once,
　　Such fortune would turn up ;
She was a kind of sorceress,
　　But studied in a cup !

IX.

So he walked up to Lady Wye,
　　And took her quite amazed,—
She thought, tho' John was tall enough,
　　He wanted to be raised.

X.

But John—for why ? she was a dame
　　Of such a dwarfish sort—
Had only come to bid her make
　　Her mourning very short.

XI.

Said he, your lord is dead and cold,
You only cry in vain ;

'*He took her quite amazed.*'
Copyright 1893 by Macmillan & Co.

Not all the cries of London now
Could call him back again !

XII.

You'll soon have many a noble beau,
    To dry your noble tears—
But just consider this, that I
    Have followed you for years.

XIII.

And tho' you are above me far,
    What matters high degree,
When you are only four foot nine,
    And I am six foot three !

XIV.

For tho' you are of lofty race,
    And I'm a low-born elf ;
Yet none among your friends could say,
    You matched beneath yourself.

XV.

Said she, such insolence as this
    Can be no common case ;
Tho' you are in my service, sir,
    Your love is out of place.

XVI.

O Lady Wyc! O Lady Wyc!
Consider what you do;
How can you be so short with me,
I am not so with you!

' *They stripped his coat, and gave him kicks.*

XVII.

Then ringing for her serving men,
They showed him to the door:
Said they, you turn out better now,
Why didn't you before?

XVIII.

They stripped his coat, and gave him kicks
    For all his wages due ;
And off, instead of green and gold,
    He went in black and blue.

'"Huzza!" the sergeant cried.'

XIX.

No family would take him in,
    Because of his discharge ;
So he made up his mind to serve
    The country all at large.

XX.

Huzza! the sergeant cried, and put
  The money in his hand,
And with a shilling cut him off
  From his paternal land.

XXI.

For when his regiment went to fight
  At Saragossa town,
A Frenchman thought he looked too tall,
  And so he cut him down!

MARY'S GHOST

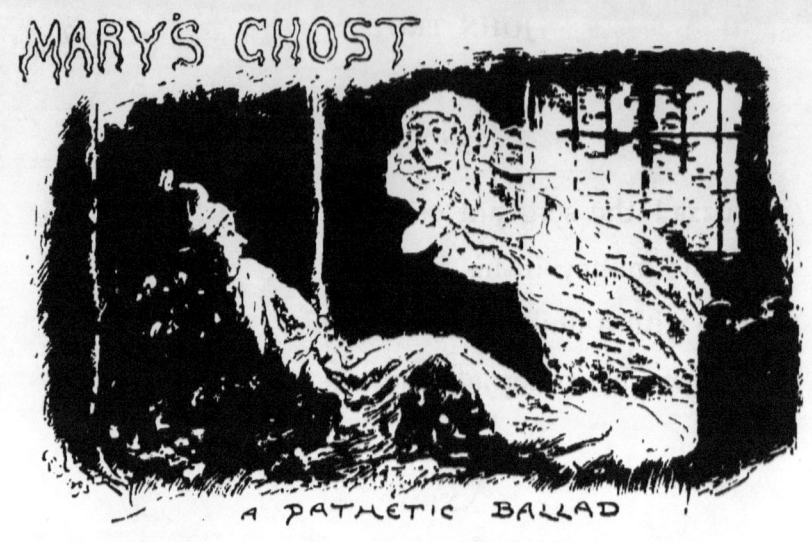

A PATHETIC BALLAD

I.

'Twas in the middle of the night,
    To sleep young William tried;
    When Mary's ghost came stealing in,
And stood at his bed-side.

II.

O William dear! O William dear!
    My rest eternal ceases;
Alas! my everlasting peace
    Is broken into pieces.

III.

I thought the last of all my cares
    Would end with my last minute;

But though I went to my long home,
I didn't stay long in it.

' *They've come and boned your Mary.*'

IV.

The body-snatchers they have come,
  And made a snatch at me;
It's very hard them kind of men
  Won't let a body be!

V.

You thought that I was buried deep,
  Quite decent like and chary,
But from her grave in Mary-bone,
  They've come and boned your Mary.

VI.

The arm that used to take your arm
  Is took to Dr. Vyse;
And both my legs are gone to walk
  The hospital at Guy's.

VII.

I vowed that you should have my hand,
  But fate gives us denial;
You'll find it there, at Dr. Bell's,
  In spirits and a phial.

VIII.

As for my feet, the little feet
  You used to call so pretty,
There's one, I know, in Bedford Row,
  The t'other's in the City.

IX.

I can't tell where my head is gone,
But Doctor Carpue can ;
As for my trunk it's all packed up
To go by Pickford's van.

' In spirits and a phial.'
Copyright 1893 by Macmillan & Co.

X.

I wish you'd go to Mr. P.
And save me such a ride ;
I don't half like the outside place,
They've took for my inside.

XI.

The cock it crows—I must be gone !
My William, we must part !
But I'll be yours in death, altho'
Sir Astley has my heart.

XII.

Don't go to weep upon my grave,
And think that there I be ;
They haven't left an atom there
Of my anatomie.

The Careleſſe Nvrſe Mayd.

SAWE a Mayd sitte on a Bank,
  Beguiled by Wooer fayne and fond !
And whiles His flatterynge Vowes She drank,
Her Nurselynge slipt within a Pond !

All Even Tide they Talkde and Kist,
For She was Fayre and He was Kinde ;
The Sunne went down before She wist
Another Sonne had sett behinde !

With angrie Hands and frownynge Browe,
That deemd Her owne the Urchine's Sinne,
She pluckt Him out, but he was nowe
Past being Whipt for fallynge in.

She then beginnes to wayle the Ladde
With Shrikes that Echo answered round—
O foolishe Mayd! to be soe sadde
The Momente that her Care was drownd!

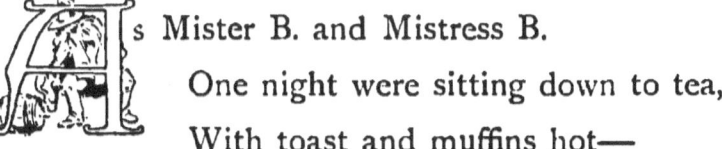

" Blow high, blow low."—*Sea Song*.

As Mister B. and Mistress B.
One night were sitting down to tea,
With toast and muffins hot—
They heard a loud and sudden bounce,
That made the very china flounce ;
They could not for a time pronounce
If they were safe or shot—
For Memory brought a deed to match
At Deptford done by night—
Before one eye appeared a Patch
In t'other eye a Blight !

To be belaboured out of life
Without some small attempt at strife,

Our nature will not grovel ;
One impulse moved both man and dame,
He seized the tongs—she did the same,
Leaving the ruffian, if he came,
The poker and the shovel.

'*Suppose the couple standing so.*'

Suppose the couple standing so,
When rushing footsteps from below
Made pulses fast and fervent,
And first burst in the frantic cat,
All steaming like a brewer's vat,
And then—as white as my cravat—
Poor Mary May, the servant !

Lord, how the couple's teeth did chatter,
Master and Mistress both flew at her,
" Speak ! Fire ? or Murder ? What's the matter ? "
Till Mary getting breath,
Upon her tale began to touch
With rapid tongue, full trotting, such
As if she thought she had too much
To tell before her death :

" We was both, ma'am, in the wash-house, ma'am,
      a-standing at our tubs,
And Mrs. Round was seconding what little things
      I rubs ;
' Mary,' says she to me, ' I say '—and there she
      stops for coughin',
' That dratted copper flue has took to smoking
      very often,
But please the pigs,'—for that's her way of swear-
      ing in a passion,
' I'll blow it up, and not be set a-coughin' in this
      fashion ! '
Well, down she takes my master's horn—I mean
      his horn for loading,

And empties every grain alive for to set the flue
　　exploding.

'Lawk, Mrs. Round!' says I, and stares, 'that
　　quantum is unproper,

'"Come," says she, quite in a huff.'

I'm sartin sure it can't not take a pound to sky a
　　copper;

You'll powder both our heads off, so I tells you,
　　with its puff,'

But she only dried her fingers, and she takes a
　　pinch of snuff.

Well, when the pinch is over—'Teach your
grandmother to suck

A powder-horn,' says she—'Well,' says I, 'I wish
you luck.'

'Up goes the copper.'

Them words sets up her back, so with her hands
upon her hips,

'Come,' says she, quite in a huff, 'come, keep
your tongue inside your lips;

Afore ever you was born, I was well used to
    things like these ;
I shall put it in the grate, and let it turn up by
    degrees.'
So in it goes, and bounce- O Lord ! it gives us
    such a rattle,
I thought we both were canonised, like sogers in
    a battle !
Up goes the copper like a squib, and us on both
    our backs,
And bless the tubs, they bundled off, and split all
    into cracks.
Well, there I fainted dead away, and might have
    been cut shorter,
But Providence was kind, and brought me to
    with scalding water.
I first looks round for Mrs. Round, and sees her
    at a distance,
As stiff as starch, and looked as dead as anything
    in existence ;
All scorched and grimed, and more than that, I
    sees the copper slap
Right on her head, for all the world like a per-
    cussion copper cap.

Well, I crooks her little fingers, and crumps them
    well up together,
As humanity pints out, and burnt her nostrums
    with a feather :
But for all as I can do, to restore her to her mortality,
She never gives a sign of a return to sensuality.
Thinks I, well there she lies, as dead as my own
    late departed mother,
Well, she'll wash no more in this world, whatever
    she does in t'other.
So I gives myself to scramble up the linens for a
    minute,
Lawk, sich a shirt ! thinks I, it's well my master
    wasn't in it ;
Oh ! I never, never, never, never, never, see a
    sight so shockin' ;
Here lays a leg, and there a leg—I mean, you
    know, a stockin'—
Bodies all slit and torn to rags, and many a
    tattered skirt,
And arms burnt off, and sides and backs all
    scotched and black with dirt ;
But as nobody was in 'em—none but—nobody
    was hurt !

Well, there I am, a-scrambling up the things, all
in a lump,
When, mercy on us! such a groan as makes my
heart to jump.
And there she is, a-lying with a crazy sort of eye,

'A-staring at the wash-house roof.'

A-staring at the wash-house roof, laid open to the
sky;
Then she beckons with a finger, and so down to
her I reaches,
And puts my ear agin her mouth to hear her
dying speeches,

For, poor soul! she has a husband and young
    orphans, as I knew ;

Well, Ma'am, you won't believe it, but it's Gospel
    fact and true,

But these words is all she whispered—' Why,
    where *is* the powder blew ? ' "

THE DUEL

A SERIOUS BALLAD

" Like the two Kings of Brentford smelling at one nosegay."

N Brentford town, of old renown,
  There lived a Mister Bray,
Who fell in love with Lucy Bell,
  And so did Mr. Clay.

To see her ride from Hammersmith,
  By all it was allowed,
Such fair outsides are seldom seen,
  Such Angels on a Cloud.

Said Mr. Bray to Mr. Clay,
　You choose to rival me,
And court Miss Bell, but there your court
　No thoroughfare shall be.

Unless you now give up your suit,
　You may repent your love ;
I who have shot a pigeon match
　Can shoot a turtle dove.

So pray before you woo her more,
　Consider what you do ;
If you pop aught to Lucy Bell—
　I'll pop it into you.

Said Mr. Clay to Mr. Bray,
　Your threats I quite explode ;
One who has been a volunteer
　Knows how to prime and load.

And so I say to you unless
　Your passion quiet keeps,
I who have shot and hit bulls' eyes,
　May chance to hit a sheep's.

Now gold is oft for silver changed,
And that for copper red ;
But these two went away to give
Each other change for lead.

'I'll pop it into you.'

But first they sought a friend apiece,
This pleasant thought to give—

When they were dead, they thus should have
Two seconds still to live.

To measure out the ground not long
  The seconds then forbore,
And having taken one rash step,
  They took a dozen more.

They next prepared each pistol-pan
  Against the deadly strife,
By putting in the prime of death
  Against the prime of life.

Now all was ready for the foes,
  But when they took their stands,
Fear made them tremble so, they found
  They both were shaking hands.

Said Mr. C. to Mr. B.,
  Here one of us may fall,
And like St. Paul's Cathedral now
  Be doomed to have a ball.

I do confess I did attach
  Misconduct to your name ;
If I withdraw the charge, will then
  Your ramrod do the same ?

'Said Mr. C. to Mr. B.'

Said Mr. B., I do agree—
  But think of Honour's Courts !
If we go off without a shot,
  There will be strange reports.

But look, the morning now is bright,
  Though cloudy it begun :
Why can't we aim above, as if
  We had called out the sun?

So up into the harmless air
  Their bullets they did send ;
And may all other duels have
  That upshot in the end !

THE SUPPER SUPERSTITION

A PATHETIC BALLAD

"Oh flesh, flesh, how art thou fishified!"—SHAKSPEARE.

I.

'TWAS twelve o'clock by Chelsea chimes,
 When all in hungry trim,
Good Mister Jupp sat down to sup
 With wife, and Kate, and Jim.

II.

Said he, " Upon this dainty cod
 How bravely I shall sup "—
When, whiter than the tablecloth,
 A GHOST came rising up !

III.

" O father dear, O mother dear,
Dear Kate, and brother Jim—
You know when some one went to sea—
Don't cry—but I am him !

IV.

" You hope some day with fond embrace
To greet your absent Jack,
But oh, I am come here to say
I'm never coming back !

V.

" From Alexandria we set sail,
With corn, and oil, and figs,
But steering ' too much Sow,' we struck
Upon the Sow and Pigs !

VI.

" The ship we pumped till we could see
Old England from the tops ;

When down she went with all our hands,
Right in the Channel's Chops.

VII.

"Just give a look in Norey's chart,
The very place it tells ;
I think it says twelve fathoms deep,
Clay bottom, mixed with shells.

VIII.

"Well, there we are till 'hands aloft,'
We have at last a call ;
The pug I had for brother Jim,
Kate's parrot too, and all.

IX.

"But oh, my spirit cannot rest
In Davy Jones's sod,
Till I've appeared to you and said—
Don't sup on that 'ere Cod !

X.

"You live on land, and little think
What passes in the sea ;
Last Sunday week, at 2 P.M.,
That Cod was picking me !

'Don't sup on that 'ere Cod.'

XI.

"Those oysters, too, that look so plump,
And seem so nicely done,

They put my corpse in many shells,
Instead of only one.

XII.

" Oh, do not eat those oysters then,
    And do not touch the shrimps ;
When I was in my briny grave,
    They sucked my blood like imps !

' To see what brutes would do.'

XIII.

" Don't eat what brutes would never eat,
    The brutes I used to pat,

They'll know the smell they used to smell,
   Just try the dog and cat!"

XIV.

The spirit fled—they wept his fate,
   And cried, Alack, alack!
At last up started brother Jim,
   " Let's try if Jack was Jack!"

XV.

They called the dog, they called the cat,
   And little kitten too,
And-down they put the Cod and sauce,
   To see what brutes would do.

XVI.

Old Tray licked all the oysters up,
   Puss never stood at crimps,
But munched the Cod—and little kit
   Quite feasted on the shrimps!

XVII.

The thing was odd, and minus Cod
  And sauce, they stood like posts ;
Oh, prudent folks, for fear of hoax,
  Put no belief in Ghosts !

FAITHLESS NELLY GRAY

GRAY

A PATHETIC BALLAD

EN BATTLE was a soldier bold,
　　And used to war's alarms ;
But a cannon ball took off his legs,
　　So he laid down his arms !

Now as they bore him off the field,
　　Said he, " Let others shoot,
For here I leave my second leg,
　　And the Forty-second Foot ! "

The army-surgeons made him limbs :
Said he,—" They're only pegs :
But there's as wooden members quite
As represent my legs ! "

Now Ben he loved a pretty maid,
Her name was Nelly Gray ;
So he went to pay her his devours
When he'd devoured his pay !

But when he called on Nelly Gray,
She made him quite a scoff ;
And when she saw his wooden legs,
Began to take them off !

" O Nelly Gray ! O Nelly Gray !
Is this your love so warm ?
The love that loves a scarlet coat
Should be more uniform ! "

She said, " I loved a soldier once,
For he was blithe and brave ;
But I will never have a man
With both legs in the grave !

"Before you had those timber toes,
Your love I did allow,
But then, you know, you stand upon
Another footing now!"

'She made him quite a scoff.'

"O Nelly Gray! O Nelly Gray!
For all your jeering speeches,

K

At duty's call I left my legs
    In Badajos's *breaches !* "

" Why then," said she, " you've lost the feet
    Of legs in war's alarms,
And now you cannot wear your shoes
    Upon your feats of arms ! "

" Oh, false and fickle Nelly Gray,
    I know why you refuse :—
Though I've no feet—some other man
    Is standing in my shoes !

" I wish I ne'er had seen your face ;
    But now a long farewell !
For you will be my death ;—alas !
    You will not be my *Nell !* "

Now when he went from Nelly Gray,
    His heart so heavy got—
And life was such a burthen grown,
    It made him take a knot !

So round his melancholy neck

A rope he did entwine,

'Some other man.'

And, for his second time in life,

Enlisted in the Line!

One end he tied around a beam
And then removed his pegs,
And, as his legs were off,—of course
He soon was off his legs!

And there he hung till he was dead
As any nail in town,—
For though distress had cut him up,
It could not cut him down!

A dozen men sat on his corpse,
  To find out why he died—
And they buried Ben in four cross-roads,
  With a *stake* in his inside !

OUR VILLAGE

BY A VILLAGER

OUR village, that's to say, not Miss Mitford's
village, but our village of Bullock's
Smithy,

Is come into by an avenue of trees, three oak pollards,
two elders, and a withy;

And in the middle there's a green, of about not ex-
ceeding an acre and a half;

It's common to all and fed off by nineteen cows, six
ponies, three horses, five asses, two foals, seven
pigs, and a calf!

Besides a pond in the middle, as is held by a sort of
common law lease,

'Right before the wicket.'
Copyright 1893 by Macmillan & Co.

And contains twenty ducks, six drakes, three ganders,
two dead dogs, four drowned kittens, and twelve
geese.

Of course the green's cropt very close, and does
famous for bowling when the little village boys
·play at cricket ;

Only some horse, or pig, or cow, or great jackass, is
    sure to come and stand right before the wicket.
There's fifty-five private houses, let alone barns and
    workshops, and pigsties, and poultry huts, and
    such-like sheds,
With plenty of public-houses—two Foxes, one Green
    Man, three Bunch of Grapes, one Crown, and
    six King's Heads.
The Green Man is reckoned the best, as the only one
    that for love or money can raise
A postilion, a blue jacket, two deplorable lame white
    horses, and a ramshackle " neat postchaise ! "
There's one parish church for all the people, whatso-
    ever may be their ranks in life or their degrees,
Except one very damp, small, dark, freezing cold,
    little Methodist Chapel of Ease ;
And close by the churchyard, there's a stonemason's
    yard, that when the time is seasonable
Will furnish with afflictions sore and marble urns and
    cherubims, very low and reasonable.
There's a cage comfortable enough ; I've been in it
    with Old Jack Jeffery and Tom Pike ;
For the Green Man next door will send you in ale,
    gin, or anything else you like.

I can't speak of the stocks, as nothing remains of
  them but the upright post ;
But the pound is kept in repairs for the sake of Cob's
  horse as is always there almost.

'The Green Man.'
Copyright 1893 by Macmillan & Co.

There s a smithy of course, where that queer sort of
  a chap in his way, Old Joe Bradley,
Perpetually hammers and stammers, for he stutters
  and shoes horses very badly.

There's a shop of all sorts that sells everything, kept
  by the widow of Mr. Task ;
But when you go there it's ten to one she's out of
  everything you ask.
You'll know her house by the swarm of boys, like
  flies, about the old sugary cask :
There are six empty houses and not so well papered
  inside as out,
For bill-stickers won't beware, but stick notices of
  sales and election placards all about.
That's the Doctor's with a green door, where the
  garden pots in the window is seen ;
A weakly monthly rose that don't blow, and a dead
  geranium, and a teaplant with five black leaves,
  and one green.
As for hollyhocks at the cottage doors, and honey-
  suckles and jasmines, you may go and whistle ;
But the Tailor's front garden grows two cabbages, a
  dock, a ha'porth of pennyroyal, two dandelions,
  and a thistle !
There are three small orchards—Mr. Busby's the
  schoolmaster's is the chief—
With two pear trees that don't bear ; one plum, and
  an apple that every year is stripped by a thief.

There's another small day-school too, kept by the
respectable Mrs. Gaby,

'A select establishment.'
Copyright 1893 by Macmillan & Co.

A select establishment for six little boys, and one
big, and four little girls and a baby ;
There's a rectory with pointed gables and strange odd
chimneys that never smokes,

For the Rector don't live on his living like other
Christian sort of folks ;

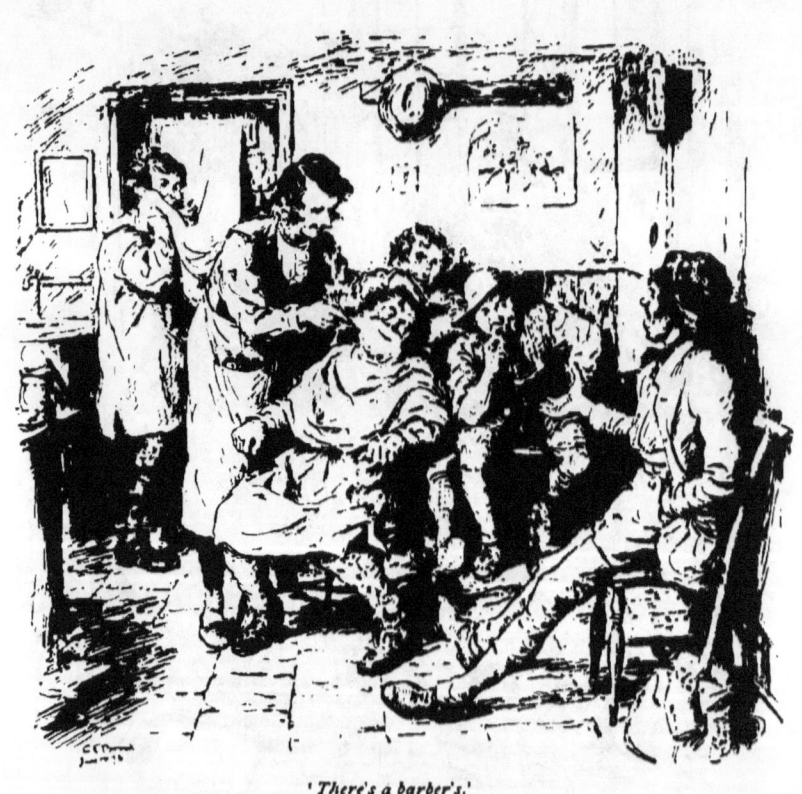

' There's a barber's.'

There's a barber's once a week well filled with rough
black-bearded, shock-headed churls,
And a window with two feminine men's heads, and
two masculine ladies in false curls ;

There's a butcher, and a carpenter's, and a plumber,
and a small greengrocer's, and a baker,

But he won't bake on a Sunday ; and there's a
sexton that's a coal merchant besides, and an
undertaker ;

And a toyshop, but not a whole one, for a village
can't compare with the London shops ;

One window sells drums, dolls, kites, carts, bats,
Clout's balls, and the other sells malt and hops.

And Mrs. Brown in domestic economy not to be a
bit behind her betters,

Lets her house to a milliner, a watchmaker, a rat-
catcher, a cobbler, lives in it herself, and it's the
post-office for letters.

Now I've gone through all the village—ay, from end
to end, save and except one more house,

But I haven't come to that—and I hope I never
shall—and that's the village Poor House !

"A day after the fair."—*Old Proverb*.

JOHN DAY he was the biggest man
    Of all the coachman kind,
With back too broad to be conceived
    By any narrow mind.

The very horses knew his weight,
    When he was in the rear,
And wished his box a Christmas box,
    To come but once a year.

Alas! against the shafts of love,
　　What armour can avail?
Soon Cupid sent an arrow through
　　His scarlet coat of mail.

The barmaid of the Crown he loved,
　　From whom he never ranged,
For though he changed his horses there,
　　His love he never changed.

He thought her fairest of all fares,
　　So fondly love prefers;
And often, among twelve outsides,
　　Deemed no outside like hers!

One day, as she was sitting down
　　Beside the porter-pump—
He came, and knelt with all his fat,
　　And made an offer plump.

Said she, my taste will never learn
　　To like so huge a man,
So I must beg you will come here
　　As little as you can.

But still he stoutly urged his suit
With vows, and sighs, and tears,

'And made an offer plump.'

Copyright 1893 by Macmillan & Co.

Yet could not pierce her heart, altho'
He drove the Dart for years.

In vain he wooed, in vain he sued,
   The maid was cold and proud,
And sent him off to Coventry,
   While on his way to Stroud.

'*He fretted all the way to Stroud.*'
Copyright 1893 by Macmillan & Co.

He fretted all the way to Stroud,
   And thence all back to town,
The course of love was never smooth,
   So his went up and down.

L

At last her coldness made him pine
To merely bones and skin,
But still he loved like one resolved
To love through thick and thin.

'I've lost my better half.'

O Mary! view my wasted back,
And see my dwindled calf;
Tho' I have never had a wife,
I've lost my better half.

Alas, in vain he still assail'd,
   Her heart withstood the dint ;
Though he had carried sixteen stone
   He could not move a flint.

Worn out, at last he made a vow
   To break his being's link ;
For he was so reduced in size,
   At nothing he could shrink.

Now some will talk in water's praise,
   And waste a deal of breath,
But John, tho' he drank nothing else,
   He drank himself to death !

The cruel maid that caused his love
   Found out the fatal close,
For looking in the butt, she saw
   The butt-end of his woes.

Some say his spirit haunts the Crown,
   But that is only talk—
For after riding all his life,
   His ghost objects to walk !

LIEUTENANT LUFF

A COMIC BALLAD

ALL you that are too fond of wine,
　　Or any other stuff,
Take warning by the dismal fate
　　Of one Lieutenant Luff.
A sober man he might have been,
　　Except in one regard,
He did not like soft water,
　　So he took to drinking hard !

Said he, " Let others fancy slops,
　　And talk in praise of Tea,

But I am no Bohemian,
　So do not like Bohea.
If wine's a poison, so is Tea,
　Though in another shape :
What matter whether one is kill'd
　By canister or grape ! "

According to this kind of taste
　Did he indulge his drouth,
And being fond of Port, he made
　A port-hole of his mouth !
A single pint he might have sipp'd
　And not been out of sorts,
In geologic phrase—the rock
　He split upon was quarts !

To " hold the mirror up to vice "
　With him was hard, alas !
The worse for wine he often was,
　But not " before a glass."
No kind and prudent friend had he
　To bid him drink no more,—
The only chequers in his course
　Were at a tavern door !

Full soon the sad effects of this

His frame began to show,

'*That old enemy the gout.*'

For that old enemy the gout

Had taken him in toe !

And join'd with this an evil came
  Of quite another sort—
For while he drank, himself, his purse
  Was getting " something short."

For want of cash he soon had pawn'd
  One half that he possessed,
And drinking showed him duplicates
  Beforehand of the rest !
So now his creditors resolved
  To seize on his assets ;
For why,—they found that his half-pay
  Did not half pay his debts.

But Luff contrived a novel mode
  His creditors to chouse ;
For his own execution he
  Put into his own house !
A pistol to the muzzle charged
  He took devoid of fear ;
Said he, " This barrel is my last,
  So now for my last bier ! "

Against his lungs he aimed the slugs,
　　And not against his brain,
So he blew out his lights—and none
　　Could blow them in again!
A Jury for a Verdict met,
　　And gave it in these terms :—
" We find as how as certain slugs
　　Has sent him to the worms!"

'Said he, " This barrel is my last."'

THE CHINA-MENDER

OOD-MORNING, Mr. What-d'ye-call !

Well ! here's another pretty job !

Lord help my Lady !—what a smash !—if you had
only heard her sob !

It was all through Mr. Lambert : but for certain he
was wincy,

To think for to go to sit down on a table full of
Chiney.

"Deuce take your stupid head !" says my Lady to
his very face ;

But politeness, you know, is nothing when there's
    Chiney in the case ;

And if ever a woman was fond of Chiney to a
    passion,

It's my mistress, and all sorts of it, whether new or
    old fashion.

Her brother's a sea-captain, and brings her home
    shiploads—

Such bonzes, and such dragons, and nasty squatting
    things like toads ;

And great nidnoddin' mandarins, with palsies in the
    head :

I declare I've often dreamt of them, and had night-
    mares in my bed.

But the frightfuller they are—lawk ! she loves them
    all the better,

She'd have Old Nick himself made of Chiney if they'd
    let her.

Lawk-a-mercy ! break her Chiney, and it's breaking
    her very heart ;

If I touched it, she would very soon say, " Mary, we
    must part."

To be sure she *is* unlucky : only Friday comes
    Master Randall,

And breaks a broken spout, and fresh chips a tea-
cup handle :

' He will so finger and touch.'

He's a dear, sweet little child, but he will so finger
and touch,

And that's why my Lady doesn't take to children
much.

'*Stupid Mr. Lambert.*'

Well, there's stupid Mr. Lambert, with his two great-
coat flaps,
Must go and sit down on the Dresden shepherdesses'
laps,

As if there was no such things as rosewood chairs in
the room !

I couldn't have made a greater sweep with the handle
of the broom.

Mercy on us ! how my mistress began to rave and
tear !

Well, after all, there's nothing like good ironstone
ware for wear.

If ever I marry, that's flat, I'm sure it won't be John
Dockery—

I should be a wretched woman in a shop full of
crockery.

I should never like to wipe it, though I love to be
neat and tidy,

And afraid of mad bulls on market-days every Monday and Friday.

I'm very much mistook if Mr. Lambert's will be a
catch ;

The breaking the Chiney will be the breaking-off of
his own match.

Missis wouldn't have an angel, if he was careless
about Chiney ;

She never forgives a chip, if it's ever so small and
tiny.

Lawk! I never saw a man in all my life in such a
taking;

I could find it in my heart to pity him for all his
mischief-making.

To see him stand a-hammering and stammering, like
a zany;

But what signifies apologies, if they won't mend old
Chaney!

If he sent her up whole crates full, from Wedgwood's
and Mr. Spode's,

He couldn't make amends for the crack'd mandarins
and smash'd toads.

Well! every one has their tastes, but, for my part,
my own self,

I'd rather have the figures on my poor dear grandmother's old shelf:

A nice pea-green poll-parrot, and two reapers with
brown ears of corns,

And a shepherd with a crook after a lamb with two
gilt horns,

And such a Jemmy Jessamy in top-boots and sky-
blue vest,

And a frill and flower'd waistcoat, with a fine bow-
pot at the breast.

'A hearty woman for her years.'

God help her, poor old soul! I shall come into 'em
at her death,

Though she's a hearty woman for her years, except
    her shortness of breath.

Well ! you may think the things will mend—if they
    won't, Lord mend us all !

My lady will go in fits, and Mr. Lambert won't need
    to call ;

I'll be bound in any money, if I had a guinea to
    give,

He won't sit down again on Chiney the longest day
    he has to live.

Poor soul ! I only hope it won't forbid his banns of
    marriage ;

Or he'd better have sat behind on the spikes of my
    Lady's carriage.

But you'll join 'em all of course, and stand poor Mr.
    Lambert's friend,

I'll look in twice a day, just to see, like, how they
    mend.

To be sure it is a sight that might draw tears from
    dogs and cats,

Here's this pretty little pagoda, now, has lost four of
    its cocked hats.

Be particular with the pagoda : and then here's this
    pretty bowl—

The Chinese Prince is making love to nothing because of this hole ;

And here's another Chinese man, with a face just
like a doll,

Do stick his pigtail on again, and just mend his
parasol.

But I needn't tell you what to do ; only do it out of
hand,

And charge whatever you like to charge—my Lady
won't make a stand.

Well ! good morning, Mr. What-d'ye-call, for it's
time our gossip ended :

And you know the proverb, the less as is said, the
sooner the Chiney's mended.

PLAYING AT SOLDIERS

"Who'll serve the King?"

AN ILLUSTRATION.

WHAT little urchin is there never
    Hath had that early scarlet fever,
  Of martial trappings caught?
Trappings well call'd—because they trap
And catch full many a country chap
  To go where fields are fought!

What little urchin with a rag
Hath never made a little flag
  (Our plate will show the manner),
And wooed each tiny neighbour still,
Tommy or Harry, Dick or Will,
  To come beneath the banner!

Just like that ancient shape of mist,
In Hamlet, crying " 'List, oh 'list ! "
  Come, who will serve the king,
And strike frog-eating Frenchmen dead,
And cut off Bonyparty's head ?—
  And all that sort of thing.

So used I, when I was a boy,
To march with military toy,
  And ape the soldier's life ;—-
And with a whistle or a hum,
I thought myself a Duke of Drum
  At least, or Earl of Fife.

With gun of tin and sword of lath,
Lord ! how I walk'd in glory's path
  With regimental mates,
By sound of trump and rub-a-dubs—-
To 'siege the washhouse—charge the tubs—
  Or storm the garden gates.

Ah me ! my retrospective soul !
As over memory's muster-roll

I cast my eyes anew,
My former comrades all the while
Rise up before me, rank and file,
And form in dim review.

'*Or storm the garden gates.*'

Ay, there they stand, and dress in line,
Lubbock, and Fenn, and David Vine,
    And dark " Jamakey Forde ! "
And limping Wood, and " Cocky Hawes,"
Our captain always made, because
    He had a *real* sword !

Long Lawrence, Natty Smart, and Soame,
Who said he had a gun at home,

' *That would hold up the flag.*

But that was all a brag ;
Ned Ryder, too, that used to sham
A prancing horse, and big Sam Lamb
That *would* hold up the flag !

Tom Anderson, and " Dunny White,"
Who never right-abouted right,
　　For he was deaf and dumb ;
Jack Pike, Jem Crack, and Sandy Gray,
And Dickey Bird, that wouldn't play
　　Unless he had the drum.　.

And Peter Holt, and Charley Jepp,
A chap that never kept the step—
　　No more did " Surly Hugh ; "
Bob Harrington, and " Fighting Jim "—
We often had to halt for him,
　　To let him tie his shoe.

" Quarrelsome Scott," and Martin Dick,
That kill'd the bantam cock, to stick
　　The plumes within his hat ;
Bill Hook, and little Tommy Grout,
That got so thump'd for calling out
　　" Eyes right ! " to " Squinting Matt."

Dan Simpson, that, with Peter Dodd,
Was always in the awkward squad,

And those two greedy Blakes
That took our money to the fair,

'And laid it out in cakes.'

To buy the corps a trumpet there,
And laid it out in cakes.

Where are they now?—an open war
With open mouth declaring for?—
　　Or fall'n in bloody fray?
Compell'd to tell the truth I am,
Their fights all ended with the sham,—
　　Their soldiership in play.

Brave Soame sends cheeses out in trucks,
And Martin sells the cock he plucks,
　　And Jepp now deals in wine;
Harrington bears a lawyer's bag,
And warlike Lamb retains his flag,
　　But on a tavern sign.

They tell me Cocky Hawes's sword
Is seen upon a broker's board:
　　And as for " Fighting Jim,"
In Bishopsgate, last Whitsuntide,
His unresisting cheek I spied
　　Beneath a Quaker brim!

Quarrelsome Scott is in the Church,
For Ryder now your eye must search

The marts of silk and lace—
Bird's drums are filled with figs, and mute,
And I—I've got a substitute
To Soldier in my place!

'*I've got a substitute.*'

LITTLE fairy comes at night,
Her eyes are blue, her hair is brown,
With silver spots upon her wings,
And from the moon she flutters down.

She has a little silver wand,
And when a good child goes to bed
She waves her wand from right to left,
And makes a circle round its head.

And then it dreams of pleasant things,
  Of fountains filled with fairy fish,
And trees that bear delicious fruit,
  And bow their branches at a wish :

Of arbours filled with dainty scents
  From lovely flowers that never fade ;
Bright flies that glitter in the sun,
  And glow-worms shining in the shade.

And talking birds with gifted tongues,
  For singing songs and telling tales,
And pretty dwarfs to show the way
  Through fairy hills and fairy dales.

But when a bad child goes to bed,
  From left to right she weaves her rings,
And then it dreams all through the night
  Of only ugly, horrid things!

Then lions come with glaring eyes,
  And tigers growl, a dreadful noise,
And ogres draw their cruel knives,
  To shed the blood of girls and boys.

And ogres draw their cruel knives.

Then stormy waves rush on to drown,
    Or raging flames come scorching round,
Fierce dragons hover in the air,
    And serpents crawl along the ground.

Then wicked children wake and weep,

And wish the long black gloom away ;

But good ones love the dark, and find

The night as pleasant as the day.

Morning Meditations

LET Taylor preach upon a morning breezy,
How well to rise while nights and larks are flying,—
For my part getting up seems not so easy
By half as *lying*.

What if the lark does carol in the sky,
Soaring beyond the sight to find him out—
Wherefore am I to rise at such a fly?
I'm not a trout.

Talk not to me of bees and such like hums,
The smell of sweet herbs at the morning prime—
Only lie long enough, and bed becomes
    A bed of *time*.

To me Dan Phœbus and his car are nought,
His steeds that paw impatiently about,—
Let them enjoy, say I, as horses ought,
    The first turn-out !

Right beautiful the dewy meads appear
Besprinkled by the rosy-finger'd girl ;
What then,—if I prefer my pillow-beer
    To early pearl ?

My stomach is not ruled by other men's,
And grumbling for a reason, quaintly begs
" Wherefore should master rise before the hens
    Have laid their eggs ? "

Why from a comfortable pillow start
To see faint flushes in the east awaken ?
A fig, say I, for any streaky part,
    Excepting bacon.

An early riser Mr. Gray has drawn,
Who used to haste the dewy grass among,
" To meet the sun upon the upland lawn "--
    Well—he died young.

' With charwomen and sweeps such early hours agree.'

With charwomen such early hours agree,
And sweeps, that earn betimes their bit and sup ;
But I'm no climbing boy, and need not be
    " All up—all up ! "

So here I'll lie, my morning calls deferring,

Till something nearer to the stroke of noon ;

A man that's fond precociously of *stirring*,

Must be a spoon.

WAS off the Wash—the sun went down — the sea looked black and grim,

For stormy clouds, with murky fleece, were mustering at the brim ;

Titanic shades! enormous gloom !—as if the solid night

Of Erebus rose suddenly to seize upon the light !

It was a time for mariners to bear a wary eye,

With such a dark conspiracy between the sea and sky !

Down went my helm—close reef'd—the tack held
freely in my hand—

With ballast snug—I put about, and scudded for the
land.

Loud hissed the sea beneath her lee—my little boat
flew fast,

But faster still the rushing storm came borne upon
the blast.

Lord! what a roaring hurricane beset the straining
sail!

What furious sleet, with level drift, and fierce assaults
of hail!

What darksome caverns yawned before! what jagged
steeps behind!

Like battle-steeds, with foamy manes, wild tossing in
the wind.

Each after each sank down astern, exhausted in the
chase,

But where it sank another rose and gallop'd in its
place;

As black as night—they turned to white, and cast
against the cloud

A snowy sheet, as if each surge upturned a sailor's
shroud:

Still flew my boat ; alas ! alas ! her course was nearly
    run !

Behold yon fatal billow rise—ten billows heap'd' in
    one !

With fearful speed the dreary mass came rolling,
    rolling fast,

As if the scooping sea contain'd one only wave at
    last !

Still on it came, with horrid roar, a swift pursuing
    grave ;

It seemed as though some cloud had turn'd its huge-
    ness to a wave !

Its briny sleet began to beat beforehand in my
    face—

I felt the rearward keel begin to climb its swelling
    base !

I saw its alpine hoary head impending over mine !

Another pulse—and down it rush'd—an avalanche
    of brine !

Brief pause had I, on God to cry, or think of wife
    and home ;

The waters closed—and when I shriek'd, I shriek'd
    below the foam !

Beyond that rush I have no hint of any after deed—

For I was tossing on the waste, as senseless as a
weed.

.   .   .   .   .

" Where am I ?—in the breathing world, or in the
world of death ? "

With sharp and sudden pang I drew another birth
of breath ;

My eyes drank in a doubtful light, my ears a doubtful sound—   .

And was that ship a *real* ship whose tackle seem'd
around ?

A moon, as if the earthly moon, was shining up aloft ;

But were those beams the very beams that I had
seen so oft ?

A face, that mocked the human face, before me
watched alone ;

But were those eyes the eyes of man that look'd
against my own ?

Oh, never may the moon again disclose me such a
sight

As met my gaze, when first I look'd, on that
accursèd night !

I've seen a thousand horrid shapes begot of fierce
    extremes

' *That Grimly One.*

Of fever ; and most frightful things have haunted in
    my dreams—
Hyenas—cats—blood-loving bats—and apes with
    hateful stare—

Pernicious snakes, and shaggy bulls—the lion, and
    she-bear—
Strong enemies, with Judas looks, of treachery and
    spite—
Detested features, hardly dimmed and banished by
    the light !
Pale-sheeted ghosts, with gory locks, upstarting from
    their tombs—
All phantasies and images that flit in midnight
    glooms—
Hags, goblins, demons, lemures, have made me all
    aghast,—
But nothing like that GRIMLY ONE who stood beside
    the mast !

His cheek was black—his brow was black—his eyes
    and hair as dark :
His hand was black, and where it touched, it left a
    sable mark ;
His throat was black, his vest the same, and when,
    I looked beneath,
His breast was black—all, all was black, except his
    grinning teeth.

His sooty crew were like in hue, as black as Afric
  slaves !
Oh horror ! e'en the ship was black that ploughed
  the inky waves !

" Alas ! " I cried, " for love of truth and blessed
  mercy's sake !
Where am I ? in what dreadful ship ? upon what
  dreadful lake ?
What shape is that, so very grim, and black as any
  coal ?
It is Mahound, the Evil One, and he has gained my
  soul !
Oh, mother dear ! my tender nurse ! dear meadows
  that beguil'd
My happy days, when I was yet a little sinless child,—
My mother dear—my native fields, I never more
  shall see :
I'm sailing in the Devil's Ship, upon the Devil's
  Sea ! "

Loud laughed that SABLE MARINER, and loudly in
  return

His sooty crew sent forth a laugh that rang from
   stem to stern—
A dozen pair of grimly cheeks were crumpled on the
   nonce—

'They crowed their fill.'

As many sets of grinning teeth came shining out at
   once :
A dozen gloomy shapes at once enjoyed the merry
   fit,
With shriek and yell, and oaths as well, like Demons
   of the Pit.

They crowed their fill, and then the Chief made
    answer for the whole ;—

" Our skins," said he, " are black, ye see, because we
    carry coal ;

You'll find your mother sure enough, and see your
    native fields—

For this here ship has picked you up—the Mary
    Ann of Shields ! "

AMONGST the sights that Mrs. Bond
        Enjoyed yet grieved at more than others,
Were little ducklings in a pond,
        Swimming about beside their mothers—
Small things like living water-lilies,
But yellow as the daffo-*dillies*.

" It's very hard," she used to moan,
        " That other people have their ducklings
To grace their waters—mine alone
        Have never any pretty chucklings."

For why!—each little yellow navy
Went down—all downy—to old Davy!

She had a lake—a pond, I mean—
    Its wave was rather thick than pearly—
She had two ducks, their napes were green—
    She had a drake, his tail was curly,—
Yet 'spite of drake, and ducks, and pond,
No little ducks had Mrs. Bond!

The birds were both the best of mothers—
    The nests had eggs—the eggs had luck—
The infant D's came forth like others—
    But there, alas! the matter stuck!
They might as well have all died addle
As die when they began to paddle!

For when, as native instinct taught her,
    The mother set her brood afloat, ·
They sank ere long right under water,
    Like any overloaded boat;
They were web-footed too to see,
As ducks and spiders ought to be!

No peccant humour in a gander
  Brought havoc on her little folks,—
No poaching cook—a frying pander
  To appetite,—destroyed their yolks,—
Beneath her very eyes, Od rot 'em !
They went, like plummets, to the bottom.

The thing was strange—a contradiction
  It seemed of nature and her works !
For little ducks, beyond conviction,
  Should float without the help of corks :
Great Johnson it bewildered him—
To hear of ducks that could not swim !

Poor Mrs. Bond ! what could she do
  But change the breed—and she tried divers
Which dived as all seemed born to do ;
  No little ones were e'er survivors—
Like those that copy gems I'm thinking,
They all were given to die-sinking !

In vain their downy coats were shorn ;
  They floundered still !—Batch after batch went !

'The thing was strange.'

The little fools seemed only born
 And hatched for nothing but a hatchment!
Whene'er they launched—oh, sight of wonder!
Like fires the water "got them under!"

No woman ever gave their lucks
   A better chance than Mrs. Bond did ;
At last quite out of heart and ducks,
   She gave her pond up, and desponded ;
For Death among the water-lilies,
Cried " *Duc* ad me " to all her dillies !

But though resolved to breed no more,
   She brooded often on this riddle—
Alas ! 'twas darker than before !
   At last about the summer's middle,
What Johnson, Mrs. Bond, or none did,
To clear the matter up the Sun did !

The thirsty Sirius, dog-like, drank
   So deep, his furious tongue to cool,
The shallow waters sank and sank,
   And lo, from out the wasted pool,
Too hot to hold them any longer,
There crawled some eels as big as conger !

I wish all folks would look a bit, ·
   In such a case below the surface ;

And when the eels were caught and split
   By Mrs. Bond, just think of *her* face,
In each inside at once to spy
   A duckling turned to giblet-pie !

'*There crawled some eels.*'

The sight at once explained the case,
   Making the Dame look rather silly,
The tenants of that *Eely Place*
   Had found the way to *Pick a dilly*,
And so, by under-water suction,
Had wrought the little ducks' abduction.

THE LOST HEIR

ONE day, as I was going by

    That part of Holborn christened High,

I heard a loud and sudden cry

    That chill'd my very blood ;

And lo ! from out a dirty alley,

Where pigs and Irish wont to rally,

I saw a crazy woman sally,

    Bedaub'd with grease and mud.

O

She turn'd her East, she turn'd her West,
Staring like Pythoness possest,
With streaming hair and heaving breast,
   As one stark mad with grief.
This way and that she wildly ran,
Jostling with woman and with man—
Her right hand held a frying pan,
   The left a lump of beef.
At last her frenzy seem'd to reach
A point just capable of speech,
And with a tone almost a screech,
   As wild as ocean birds,
Or female Ranter mov'd to preach,
   She gave her " sorrow words."
" Oh Lord ! oh dear, my heart will break, I shall go
   stick stark staring wild !
Has ever a one seen anything about the streets like
   a crying lost-looking child ?
Lawk help me, I don't know where to look, or to run,
   if I only knew which way—
A child as is lost about London streets, and especially
   Seven Dials, is a needle in a bottle of hay.
I am all in a quiver—get out of my sight, do, you
   wretch, you little Kitty M'Nab !

You promised to have half an eye to him, you know
you did, you dirty deceitful young drab.

The last time as ever I see him, poor thing, was with
my own blessed motherly eyes,

Sitting as good as gold in the gutter, a-playing at
making little dirt pies.

I wonder he left the court where he was better off
than all the other young boys,

With two bricks, an old shoe, nine oyster-shells, and
a dead kitten by way of toys.

When his Father comes home, and he always comes
home as sure as ever the clock strikes one,

He'll be rampant, he will, at his child being lost ; and
the beef and the inguns not done !

La bless you, good folks, mind your own consarns,
and don't be making a mob in the street ;

Oh   Serjeant   M'Farlane !   you   have   not   come
across my poor little boy, have you, in your
beat ?

Do, good people, move on ! don't stand staring at me
like a parcel of stupid stuck pigs ;

Saints forbid ! but he's p'r'aps been inviggled away
up a court for the sake of his clothes by the
prigs ;

He'd a very good jacket, for certain, for I bought it
    myself for a shilling one day in Rag Fair ;

'Oh Serjeant M'Farlane !'

And his trousers considering not very much patch'd,
    and red plush, they was once his Father's best
    pair.
His shirt, it's very lucky I'd got washing in the tub,
    or that might have gone with the rest ;

But he'd got on a very good pinafore with only two
slits and a burn on the breast.

He'd a goodish sort of hat, if the crown was sew'd in,
and not quite so much jagg'd at the brim,

With one shoe on, and the other shoe is a boot,
and not a fit, and you'll know by that if it's
him.

Except being so well dress'd my mind would mis-
give, some old beggar woman in want of an
orphan,

Had borrow'd the child to go a-begging with, but I'd
rather see him laid out in his coffin!

Do, good people, move on, such a rabble of boys!
I'll break every bone of 'em I come near,

Go home—you're spilling the porter—go home—
Tommy Jones, go along home with your beer.

This day is the sorrowfullest day of my life, ever since
my name was Betty Morgan,

Them vile Savoyards! they lost him once before all
along of following a monkey and an organ.

Oh my Billy—my head will turn right round—if he's
got kiddynapp'd with them Italians,

They'll make him a plaster parish image boy, they
will, the outlandish tatterdemalions.

Billy—where are you, Billy? I'm as hoarse as a
crow, with screaming for ye, you young sorrow!

'Playing like angels.'

And shan't have half a voice, no more I shan't, for
crying fresh herrings to-morrow.
Oh Billy, you're bursting my heart in two, and my
life won't be of no more vally,
If I'm to see other folks' darlin's, and none of mine,
playing like angels in our alley.

And what shall I do but cry out my eyes, when I
looks at the old three-legged chair

As Billy used to make coach and horses of, and there
a'n't no Billy there !

I would run all the wide world over to find him, if I
only know'd where to run,

Little Murphy, now I remember, was once lost for a
month through stealing a penny bun,—

The Lord forbid of any child of mine ! I think it
would kill me railey,

To find my Bill holdin' up his little innocent hand at
the Old Bailey.

For though I say it as oughtn't, yet I will say, you
may search for miles and mileses,

And not find one better brought up, and more pretty
behaved, from one end to t'other of St. Giles's.

And if I called him a beauty, it's no lie, but only as
a mother ought to speak ;

You never set eyes on a more handsomer face, only
it hasn't been washed for a week ;

As for hair, tho' it's red, it's the most nicest hair when
I've time to just show it the comb ;

I'll owe 'em five pounds, and a blessing besides, as
will only bring him safe and sound home.

He's blue eyes, and not to be call'd a squint, though
    a little cast he's certainly got ;

And his nose is still a good un, tho' the bridge is
    broke, by his falling on a pewter pint pot ;

He's got the most elegant wide mouth in the world,
    and very large teeth for his age ;

And quite as fit as Mrs. Murdockson's child to play
    Cupid on the Drury Lane stage.

And then he has got such dear winning ways—
    but oh, I never never shall see him no
    more !

Oh dear ! to think of losing him just after nursing
    him back from death's door !

Only the very last month when the windfalls, hang
    'em, was at twenty a penny !

And the threepence he'd got by grottoing was
    spent in plums, and sixty for a child is too
    many.

And the cholera man came and whitewash'd us all,
    and, drat him, made a seize of our hog.

It's no use to send the Crier to cry him about, he's
    such a blunderin' drunken old dog ;

The last time he was fetched to find a lost child, he
    was guzzling with his bell at the Crown,

And went and cried a boy instead of a girl, for a
distracted Mother and Father about Town.

Billy—where are you, Billy, I say ? come Billy, come
home, to your best of mothers !

I'm scared when I think of them cabroleys, they
drive so, they'd run over their own Sisters and
Brothers.

Or may be he's stole by some chimbly-sweeping
wretch, to stick fast in narrow flues and what
not,

And be poked up behind with a picked pointed pole,
when the soot has ketch'd, and the chimbly's
red hot.

Oh I'd give the whole wide world, if the world was
mine, to clap my two longin' eyes on his
face.

For he's my darlin' of darlin's, and if he don't soon
come back, you'll see me drop stone dead on
the place.

I only wish I'd got him safe in these two motherly
arms, and wouldn't I hug him and kiss him !

Lawk ! I never knew what a precious he was—but a
child don't not feel like a child till you miss
him.

Why there he is! Punch and Judy hunting, the
    young wretch, it's that Billy as sartin as sin!
But let me get him home, with a good grip of his
    hair, and I'm blest if he shall have a whole bone
    in his skin!"

THE ASSISTANT DRAPER'S PETITION

PITY the sorrows of a class of men,
Who, though they bow to fashion and
frivolity,
No fancied claims or woes fictitious pen,
But wrongs ell-wide, and of a lasting quality.

Oppress'd and discontented with our lot,
Amongst the clamorous we take our station ;
A host of Ribbon men—yet is there not
One piece of Irish in our agitation.

We do revere Her Majesty the Queen ;
We venerate our Glorious Constitution ;
We joy King William's advent should have been,
And only want a Counter Revolution.

'Tis not Lord Russell and his final measure,
'Tis not Lord Melbourne's counsel to the throne,
'Tis not this Bill, or that, gives us displeasure,
The measures we dislike are all our own.

The Cash Law the " Great Western " loves to name,
The tone our foreign policy pervading ;
The Corn Laws—none of these we'care to blame,—
Our evils we refer to over-trading.

By tax or Tithe our murmurs are not drawn ;
We reverence the Church—but hang the cloth !
We love her ministers—but curse the lawn !
We have, alas ! too much to do with both !

We love the sex ;—to serve them is a bliss !
We trust they find us civil, never surly ;

All that we hope of female friends is this,
That their last linen may be wanted early.

Ah! who can tell the miseries of men
That serve the very cheapest shops in town?
Till faint and weary, they leave off at ten,
Knock'd up by ladies beating of 'em down!

But has not Hamlet his opinion given—
O Hamlet had a heart for Drapers' servants!
" That custom is "—say custom after seven—
" More honour'd in the breach than the observance."

O come then, gentle ladies, come in time,
O'erwhelm our counters, and unload our shelves ;
Torment us all until the seventh chime,
But let us have the remnant to ourselves !

We wish of knowledge to lay in a stock,
And not remain in ignorance incurable ;—
To study Shakespeare, Milton, Dryden, Locke,
And other fabrics that have proved so durable.

We long for thoughts of intellectual kind,
And not to go bewilder'd to our beds ;
With stuff and fustian taking up the mind,
And pins and needles running in our heads !

'For oh ! the brain gets very dull and dry.'

For oh ! the brain gets very dull and dry,
Selling from morn till night for cash or credit ;
Or with a vacant face and vacant eye,
Watching cheap prints that Knight did never edit.

Till sick with toil, and lassitude extreme,

We often think, when we are dull and vapoury,

The bliss of Paradise was so supreme,

Because that Adam did not deal in drapery.

THE VOLUNTEER

"The clashing of my armour in my ears
  Sounds like a passing bell ; my buckler puts me
  In mind of a bier : this, my broadsword, a pickaxe
  To dig my grave."—*The Lover's Progress.*

I.

IT WAS in that memorable year
    France threatened to put off in
    Flat-bottomed boats, intending each
To be a British coffin,
To make sad widows of our wives,
And every babe an orphan :—

II.

When coats were made of scarlet cloaks,
And heads were dredged with flour,
I 'listed in the Lawyers' Corps,
Against the battle hour ;
A perfect Volunteer—for why ?
I brought my " will and pow'r."

III.

One dreary day—a day of dread,
Like Cato's, over-cast—
About the hour of six (the morn
And I were breaking fast),
There came a loud and sudden sound,
That struck me all aghast !

IV.

A dismal sort of morning roll,
That was not to be eaten :
Although it was no skin of mine
But parchment that was beaten,
I felt tattooed through all my flesh,
Like any Otaheitan.

P

V.

My jaws with utter dread enclosed
The morsel I was munching,
And terror locked them up so tight,
My very teeth went crunching
All through my bread and tongue at once,
Like sandwich made at lunching.

VI.

My hand that held the teapot fast,
Stiffened, but yet unsteady,
Kept pouring, pouring, pouring o'er
The cup in one long eddy,
Till both my hose were marked with *tea,*
As they were marked already.

VII.

I felt my visage turn from red
To white—from cold to hot ;
But it was nothing wonderful
My colour changed, I wot,
For, like some variable silks,
I felt that I was shot.

VIII.

And looking forth with anxious eye,
From my snug upper story,

'*Looking forth with anxious eye.*'

I saw our melancholy corps
Going to beds all gory ;
The pioneers seemed very loth
To axe their way to glory.

IX.

The captain marched as mourners march,
The ensign too seemed lagging,
And many more, although they were
No ensigns, took to flagging—
Like corpses in the Serpentine,
Methought they wanted dragging.

X.

But while I watched, the thought of death
Came like a chilly gust,
And lo! I shut the window down,
With very little lust
To join so many marching men,
That soon might be March dust.

XI.

Quoth I, " Since Fate ordains it so,
Our foe the coast must land on ; "
I felt so warm beside the fire
I cared not to abandon ;
Our hearths and homes are always things
That patriots make a stand on.

XII.

" The fools that fight abroad for home,"
Thought I, " may get a wrong one ;
Let those that have no home at all
Go battle for a long one."
The mirror here confirmed me this
Reflection, by a strong one :

XIII.

For there, where I was wont to shave,
And deck me like Adonis,
There stood the leader of our foes,
With vultures for his cronies—
No Corsican, but Death itself,
The Bony of all Bonies.

XIV.

A horrid sight it was, and sad,
To see the grisly chap
Put on my crimson livery,
And then begin to clap
My helmet on—ah me ! it felt
Like any felon's cap.

XV.

My plume seemed borrowed from a hearse,
An undertaker's crest ;

'The mirror here confirmed me this.'

My epaulettes like coffin-plates ;
My belt so heavy press'd,

Four pipeclay cross-roads seem'd to lie
At once upon my breast.

XVI.

My brazen breastplate only lack'd
A little heap of salt,
To make me like a corpse full dress'd,
Preparing for the vault—
To set up what the Poet calls
My everlasting halt.

XVII.

This funeral show inclined me quite
To peace :—and here I am !
Whilst better lions go to war,
Enjoying with the lamb
A lengthen'd life, that might have been
A Martial Epigram.

" 'Twa dogs, that were na thrang at hame,
Forgather'd ance upon a time."—BURNS.

ONE morn—it was the very morn
September's sportive month was born—
The hour, about the sunrise, early :
The sky grey, sober, still, and pearly,
With sundry orange streaks and tinges
Through daylight's door, at cracks and hinges ;

The air calm, bracing, freshly cool,

As if just skimm'd from off a pool ;

The scene, red, russet, yellow, leaden,

From stubble, fern, and leaves that deaden,

Save here and there a turnip patch,

Too verdant with the rest to match ;

And far a-field a hazy figure,

Some roaming lover of the trigger.

Meanwhile the level light perchance

Pick'd out his barrel with a glance ;

For all around a distant popping

Told birds were flying off or dropping.

Such was the morn—a morn right fair

To seek for covey or for hare—

When, lo ! too far from human feet

For even Ranger's boldest beat,

A Dog, as in some doggish trouble,

Came cant'ring through the crispy stubble,

With dappled head in lowly droop,

But not the scientific stoop ;

And flagging, dull, desponding ears,

As if they had been soaked in tears,

And not the beaded dew that hung

The filmy stalks and weeds among,

His pace, indeed, seemed not to know
An errand, why, or where to go,
To trot, to walk, or scamper swift—
In short, he seemed a dog adrift;

' He seemed a dog adrift.'

His very tail, a listless thing,
With just an accidental swing,
Like rudder to the ripple veering,
When nobody on board is steering.
So, dull and moody, cantered on
Our vagrant pointer, christen'd Don;

When, rising o'er a gentle slope,
That gave his view a better scope,
He spied, some dozen furrows distant,
But in a spot as inconsistent,
A second dog across his track,
Without a master to his back ;
As if for wages, workman-like,
The sporting breed had made a strike,
Resolved nor birds nor puss to seek,
Without another paunch a week !

This other was a truant curly,
But, for a spaniel, wondrous surly ;
Instead of curvets gay and brisk,
He slouched along without a frisk,
With dogged air, as if he had
A good half mind to running mad ;
Mayhap the shaking at his ear
Had been a quaver too severe ;
Mayhap the whip's " exclusive dealing "
Had too much hurt e'en spaniel feeling,
Nor if he had been cut, 'twas plain
He did not mean to come again.

Of course the pair soon spied each other ;
But neither seemed to own a brother ;
The course on both sides took a curve,
As dogs when shy are apt to swerve ;
But each o'er back and shoulder throwing
A look to watch the other's going,
Till, having cleared sufficient ground,
With one accord they turned them round,
And squatting down, for forms not caring,
At one another fell to staring ;
As if not proof against a touch
Of what plagues humankind so much,
A prying itch to get at notions
Of all their neighbours' looks and motions.
Sir Don at length was first to rise—
The better dog in point of size,
And, snuffing all the ground between,
Set off, with easy jaunty mien ;
While Dash, the stranger, rose to greet him,
And made a dozen steps to meet him—
Their noses touch'd, and rubbed awhile
(Some savage nations use the style),
And then their tails a wag began,
Though on a very cautious plan,

But in their signals quantum suff.
To say " A civil dog enough."

Thus having held out olive branches,
They sank again, though not on haunches,

'Some savage nations use the style.'

But couchant, with their under jaws
Resting between the two forepaws,
The prelude, on a luckier day,
Or sequel, to a game of play :
But now they were in dumps, and thus

Began their worries to discuss,
The pointer, coming to the point
The first, on times so out of joint.
" Well, Friend,—so here's a new September
As fine a first as I remember ;
And, thanks to such an early Spring,
Plenty of birds, and strong on wing."

" Birds ! " cried the crusty little chap,
As sharp and sudden as a snap,
" A weasel suck them in the shell !
What matter birds, or flying well,
Or fly at all, or sporting weather,
If fools with guns can't hit a feather ! "

" Ay, there's the rub, indeed," said Don,
Putting his gravest visage on ;
" In vain we beat our beaten way,
And bring our *organs* into play,
Unless the proper killing kind
Of *barrel tunes* are played behind :
But when *we* shoot—that's me and Squire—
We hit as often as we fire."

" More luck for you ! " cried little Woolly,
Who felt the cruel contrast fully ;
" More luck for you, and Squire to boot !
We miss as often as we shoot ! "

' Putting his gravest visage on.'

" Indeed !—No wonder you're unhappy !
I thought you looking rather snappy ;
But fancied, when I saw you jogging,
You'd had an overdose of flogging ;
Or p'raps the gun its range had tried
While you were ranging rather wide."

" Me! running—running wide—and hit!
Me shot! what, pepper'd!—Deuce a bit!
I almost wish I had!   That Dunce,
My master, then would hit for once!
Hit me! Lord, how you talk! why zounds!
He couldn't hit a pack of hounds!"

" Well, that must be a case provoking.
What, *never*—but, you dog, you're joking!
I see a sort of wicked grin
About your jaw you're keeping in."
" A joke! an old tin kettle's clatter
Would be as much a joking matter.
To tell the truth, that dog-disaster
Is just the type of me and master,
When fagging over hill and dale,
With his vain rattle at my tail.
Bang, bang, and bang, the whole day's run,
But *leading* nothing but his gun—
The very shot, I fancy, hisses,
It's sent upon such awful misses."

" Of course it does!   But perhaps the fact is
Your master's hand is out of practice!"

" Practice ?—No doctor, where you will,
Has finer—but he cannot kill !
These three years past, thro' furze and furrow,
All covers I have hunted thorough ;

' About the moors.'

Flush'd cocks and snipes about the moors ;
And put up hares by scores and scores ;
Coveys of birds, and lots of pheasants ;—-
Yes, game enough to send in presents
To ev'ry friend he has in town,
Provided he had knock'd it down :

Q

But no—the whole three years together,
He has not giv'n me flick or feather—
For all that I have had to do
I wish I had been missing too!"

"Well,—such a hand would drive me mad ;
But is he truly quite so bad?"

"Bad!—worse!—you cannot underscore him ;
If I could put up, just before him,
The great Balloon that paid the visit
Across the water, he would miss it!
Bite him! I do believe, indeed,
It's in his very blood and breed!
It marks his life, and runs all through it ;
What can be miss'd, he's sure to do it.
Last Monday he came home to Tooting,
Dog-tired, as if he'd been a-shooting,
And kicks at me to vent his rage—
'Get out!' says he—'I've miss'd the stage!'
Of course, thought I—what chance of hitting?
You'd miss the Norwich waggon, sitting!"

" Why, he must be the county's scoff!

He ought to leave, and not let, off!

'To vent his rage.'

As fate denies his shooting wishes,

Why don't he take to catching fishes?

Or any other sporting game,

That don't require a bit of aim?"

Q 2

" Not he !—Some dogs of human kind
Will hunt by sight, because they're blind,
My master angle !—no such luck !
There he might strike, who never struck !
My master shoots because he can't,
And has an eye that aims aslant ;
Nay, just by way of making trouble,
He's changed his single gun for double ;
And now, as girls a-walking do,
His *misses* go by two and two !
I wish he had the mange, or reason
As good, to miss the shooting season !"

" Why yes, it must be main unpleasant
To point to covey, or to pheasant ;
For snobs, who, when the point is mooting,
Think *letting fly* as good as shooting !"

" Snobs !—if he'd wear his ruffled shirts,
Or coats with water-wagtail skirts,
Or trowsers in the place of smalls,
Or those tight fits he wears at balls,
Or pumps, and boots with tops, mayhap,
Why we might pass for Snip and Snap,

And shoot like blazes! fly or sit,
And none would stare, unless we hit.
But no—to make the more combustion,

'*For keepers, shy of such encroachers.*'

He goes in gaiters and in fustian,
Like Captain Ross, or Topping Sparks,
And deuce a miss but some one marks!
For keepers, shy of such encroachers,

Dog us about like common poachers !
Many's the covey I've gone by,
When underneath a sporting eye ;
Many a puss I've twigg'd, and pass'd her—
I miss 'em to prevent my master !"

" And so should I, in such a case !
There's nothing feels so like disgrace,
Or gives you such a scurvy look—
A kick and pail of slush from Cook,
Cleftsticks, or kettle, all in one,
As standing to a missing gun !
It's whirr ! and bang ! and off you bound,
To catch your bird before the ground ;
But no—a pump and ginger pop
As soon would get a bird to drop !
So there you stand, quite struck a-heap,
Till all your tail is gone to sleep ;
A sort of stiffness in your nape,
Holding your head well up to gape ;
While off go birds across the ridges,
First small as flies, and then as midges,
Cocksure, as they are living chicks,
Death's Door is not at Number Six !"

" Yes ! yes ! and then you look at master,

The cause of all the late disaster,

Who gives a stamp, and raps an oath

'*And raps an oath.*'

At gun, or birds, or maybe both ;

P'raps curses you, and all your kin,

To raise the hair upon your skin !

Then loads, rams down, and fits new caps,

To go and hunt for more miss-haps ! "

" Yes ! yes ! but, sick and sad, you feel
But one long wish to go to heel ;
You cannot scent, for cutting mugs—
Your nose is turning up, like Pug's ;
You can't hold up, but plod and mope ;
Your tail like sodden end of rope,
That o'er a wind-bound vessel's side
Has soak'd in harbour, tide and tide.
On thorns and scratches, till that moment
Unnoticed, you begin to comment ;
You never felt such bitter brambles,
Such heavy soil, in all your rambles !
You never felt your fleas so vicious !
Till, sick of life so unpropitious,
You wish at last, to end the passage,
That you were dead, and in your sassage ! "

" Yes ! that's a miss from end to end !
But, zounds ! you draw so well, my friend,
You've made me shiver, skin and gristle,
As if I heard my master's whistle !
Though how you came to learn the knack—
I thought your squire was quite a crack ! "

" And so he is !—He always hits—
And sometimes hard, and all to bits.
But ere with him our tongues we task,
I've still one little thing to ask ;
Namely, with such a random master,
Of course you sometimes want a plaster ?
Such missing hands make game of more
Than ever passed for game before—
A pounded pig—a widow's cat—
A patent ventilating hat—
For shot, like mud, when thrown so thick,
Will find a coat whereon to stick ! "

" What ! accidentals, as they're term'd ?
No, never—none—since I was worm'd—
Not e'en the Keeper's fatted calves,—
My master does not miss by halves !
His shot are like poor orphans, hurl'd
Abroad upon the whole wide world,—
But whether they be blown to dust,
As oftentimes I think they must,
Or melted down too near the sun,
What comes of them is known to none—

I never found, since I could bark,
A Barn that bore my master's mark!"

" Is that the case?—why then, my brother,
Would we could swap with one another!
Or take the Squire, with all my heart,
Nay, all my liver, so we part!
He'll hit you hares—(he uses cartridge)
He'll hit you cocks—he'll hit a partridge ;
He'll hit a snipe—he'll hit a pheasant ;
He'll hit—he'll hit whatever's present ;
He'll always hit,—as that's your wish—
His pepper never lacks a dish!"

" Come, come, you banter—let's be serious ;
I'm sure that I am half delirious,
Your picture set me so a-sighing—
But does he shoot so well—shoot flying?"

" Shoot flying? Yes—and running, walking,—
I've seen him shoot two farmers talking—
He'll hit the game, whene'er he can,
But failing that he'll hit a man,
A boy—a horse's tail or head—

Or make a pig a pig of lead,—
Oh, friend ! they say no dog as yet,
However hot, was known to sweat,
But sure I am that I perspire
Sometimes *before my master's fire !*
Misses ! no, no, he *always* hits,
But so as puts me into fits !
He shot my fellow dog this morning,
Which seemed to me sufficient warning ! "

" Quite, quite enough !—So that's a hitter !
Why, my own fate I thought was bitter,
And full excuse for cut and run ;
But give me still the missing gun !
Or rather, Sirius ! send me this,
No gun at all, to hit or miss,
Since sporting seems to shoot thus double,
That right or left it brings us trouble ! "

So ended Dash ;—and Pointer Don
Prepared to urge the moral on ;
But here a whistle long 'and shrill
Came sounding o'er the council hill,
And starting up, as if their tails

Had felt the touch of shoes and nails,
Away they scamper'd down the slope,
As fast as other pairs elope,—
Resolv'd, instead of sporting rackets,
To 'beg, or dance in fancy jackets ;
At butchers' shops to try their luck ;
To help to draw a cart or truck ;
Or lead Stone Blind poor men, at most
Who would but hit or miss a post."